"Answer me, Mia. Do you know this child?"

Mia jerked away, stung and ashamed.

What was she doing playing right into the hands of her enemy? Rocco no longer had sexual power over her, so why was she standing there, gazing up at him like...like...

She took a hasty step back, tried to remain calm as her gaze dropped to the picture. A cherubic face smiled back at her with cheeky impertinence. The child's dark blue eyes twinkled with mirth and the mop of black curls danced in a slight breeze. She wanted to reach out and caress the slightly dimpled chin, which someday would deepen like his father's.

Did she know this child?

Of course she knew him.

She'd carried him in her womb for nine months, loved him with every fiber of her being long before he'd delivered the first of many vicious kicks inside her and adored every strand of hair, every soft velvety inch of him from the moment he was placed in her arms.

Maya Blake's hopes of becoming a writer were born when she picked up her first romance at thirteen. Little did she know her dream would come true! Does she still pinch herself every now and then to make sure it's not a dream? Yes, she does! Feel free to pinch her, too, via Twitter, Facebook or Goodreads! Happy reading!

Books by Maya Blake

Harlequin Presents

Pregnant at Acosta's Demand
The Sultan Demands His Heir
His Mistress by Blackmail
An Heir for the World's Richest Man
Kidnapped for His Royal Heir

Conveniently Wed!

Crown Prince's Bought Bride

One Night With Consequences

The Boss's Nine-Month Negotiation

Bound to the Desert King

Sheikh's Pregnant Cinderella

The Notorious Greek Billionaires

Claiming My Hidden Son
Bound by My Scandalous Pregnancy

Visit the Author Profile page
at Harlequin.com for more titles.

Maya Blake

THE SICILIAN'S BANISHED BRIDE

(H) HARLEQUIN®
PRESENTS®

Recycling programs
for this product may
not exist in your area.

ISBN-13: 978-1-335-14887-2

The Sicilian's Banished Bride

Copyright © 2020 by Maya Blake

This edition published by arrangement with Harlequin Books S.A.

For questions and comments about the quality of this book,
please contact us at CustomerService@Harlequin.com.

Harlequin Enterprises ULC
22 Adelaide St. West, 40th Floor
Toronto, Ontario M5H 4E3, Canada
www.Harlequin.com

Printed in U.S.A.

THE SICILIAN'S BANISHED BRIDE

CHAPTER ONE

'HE'S YOURS, ROCCO. Find him...find him!'

The words pounded a relentless refrain in Rocco Vitelli's head as his Gulfstream sped him in the opposite direction towards a destination that had been nowhere on his itinerary when he'd woken up that morning.

The photograph in his hand shook and he tightened his grip.

Impossible.

His grandmother's words were simply...impossible.

Didn't they say everyone had a twin somewhere in the world? *Dio*, even that extrapolation was too far-fetched. This picture was of a child. He was a grown man of thirty-three. This child had nothing to do with him. Nothing...

'We'll be landing shortly, *signor.* Is there anything you require?' his attendant enquired.

Inform the pilot that I wish to change course immediately, he wanted to say. He held his tongue, his grandmother's pale face etched in anguish fresh in his mind.

Jaw clenching, he closed his fist over the picture, hiding it from sight. Unfortunately, Nonna's distressing words weren't so easy to dismiss.

'He's yours. Find him!'

Ridiculous. If he had a son, a flesh and blood extension of him somewhere in this world, he would know... wouldn't he?

A sudden wave of long-suppressed yearning swept through him, stealing his breath.

He would know. He was strict about taking precautions with his sexual partners. None of his liaisons in the recent past had lasted longer than a few weeks. And, by strict choice, none of them had been English.

He hadn't set foot in England in years and he hadn't taken an English lover since—

'Signor?'

He sighed. 'No, *grazie*.'

Just this once, he promised himself grimly. His grandmother rarely asked him for anything, not because he'd refuse, but because she insisted she needed nothing but the roof he'd provided over her head. After everything she'd sacrificed for him, running this fool's errand, even though it lodged a fist of remembered bitterness in his gut, was necessary if only to reassure her.

This visit would be short, however. Whoever this child was, Rocco intended his presence in its life to be very brief indeed.

'Has the driver been apprised of our destination?' he asked.

'*Sì, signor.* I emailed the details immediately after take-off.'

Satisfied, he nodded. Barring traffic, he should be back in the air within a few short hours. A quick detour via his Palermo villa to reassure Nonna there was no mysterious great-grandchild to be distressed about, and he could return to Abu Dhabi to oversee the final phase of the children's hospital his company was building.

Wheels touched down with barely a bump. Before it had rolled to a stop, he was moving towards the exit. His car waited on the tarmac and he slid into the back seat, grateful for its warm interior. It was early autumn, yet the temperature was near freezing.

Easing back in his seat, he glanced once more at the photo. The cherubic features, the strange, yet familiar blue eyes of the child sent another stab of deep yearning through him.

No. He wouldn't think of the past. Of *her*. The past was done, buried—

I don't want your baby!

He clenched his teeth against the chilling words slicing through his thoughts. Why were memories he'd successfully expunged for years resurfacing, today of all days?

Grimly, he shoved the photo into his breast pocket and turned his thoughts to his grandmother.

Her hysteria over the billboard picture she'd spotted on the way to morning mass was beyond his understanding. Nonna had collapsed on the pavement, much to the distress of her companion, and no amount of reassurance had soothed her except Rocco's promise, once he'd rushed to her side, that he would verify the child's identity immediately.

So here he was, on what could only be politely described as a wild goose chase. He stifled a dark curse and looked up at his driver's discreet cough.

'The news reports gridlocked traffic ahead, sir. I'll

have to take a different route if you're to keep your schedule.'

Rocco's mood darkened further. With every fibre of his being, he wished himself elsewhere. But he'd made his grandmother a promise. He'd keep it, even if it meant being in the same country, breathing the same air as that… Jezebel.

He inhaled, brought his feelings under control.

'Take whatever route you must. But make sure it's quick.'

Mia Gallagher stole another indulgent caress of her sleeping son's soft cheek before stepping away with a wry smile. Nap time was fast becoming a battle of wills. At two and a half, Gianni was vigorously resisting taking his much-needed naps. This afternoon he'd hidden behind his bedroom door, unaware his chubby legs were clearly visible through the gap in the door frame. How he managed to keep so still at his age astounded her.

Her smile slipped.

She knew exactly how he came by that particular trait. The man whose blood ran through her son's veins possessed that formidable knack, after all—

No, she wasn't going to think about him. Not now, not ever, if she could help it.

She shut the bedroom door with a sigh of relief. With an hour to herself before he woke, she had enough time to tackle the laundry and start dinner.

The sound of the doorbell as she approached her small living room made her heart sink.

Mrs Hart.

With her financial juggling getting trickier by the

day and another of Gianni's photo shoots cancelled—
the third one in two weeks—the last thing Mia needed
was her neighbour's nosiness disguised as friendly concern. For a moment, she considered not answering.

The doorbell pealed again, followed by an insistent
knock.

Mrs Hart had probably seen them return from the
park. Mia had no choice but to answer or risk Gianni
waking up.

She pulled open the door, a firm but polite excuse on
her lips, only to take a horrified step back, her words
choking in her throat as a painfully familiar figure filled
the doorway.

Rocco reeled with the shock of coming face to face with
the woman he'd banished from his life three years ago,
even as the molten burn of instant lust thickened the
blood roaring through his veins.

'*Cosa è questo?*' He wasn't sure whether he questioned his body's unwelcome reaction to her or the fact
that someone in his security team had made a fatal
blunder when he'd asked for the location of the child
in the photo. Because this had to be an inexcusable,
colossal error.

The breath he sucked in did nothing to provide clar-
ity.

Someone's head…hell, several heads, would roll for
delivering him to the last person on earth he wished
to encounter; the one person he'd sworn never to even
think of, ever again!

He conducted a swift scrutiny of Mia Gallagher and
experienced a fresh jolt of shock.

Gone was the sleekly coiffed, elegant and voluptuous woman who'd graced his boardroom and bedroom for several months over three years ago. Gone were the thigh-skimming designer suits and the stunningly made-up face that had held him in thrall for far longer than he'd deemed wise, even then.

This woman looked pale and shadows lurked under her eyes, rendering the once vibrant depths a dull green. Her honey-blonde hair, scraped back in a utilitarian ponytail, lacked its former lustre. Her face was devoid of make-up, and her mouth, now hanging open, although still full and sensually curved, was bare of gloss.

His gaze lowered, and he frowned. She'd lost weight but, somehow, her breasts seemed fuller, heavier than he remembered. Lower still, her long legs were covered by pair of baggy shapeless jeans.

Altogether an unattractive package, and far removed from the sensual bombshell he'd lusted after... and nearly lost his mind over?

He jerked back at the hard, unexpected kick in his groin.

Don't even go there!

His gaze flicked back to her face and Rocco forced himself to dismiss the twisting current of sexual tension that gripped him. What interested him was discovering who had brought him here, to this woman.

He reached for his phone, then paused when he glimpsed the look on her face. Surely that wasn't... panic?

'Of course.' Why hadn't he realised it before? There was no else involved. She'd orchestrated this meeting.

And now, faced with his visible anger, she was panicking.

Dio, her audacity astounded him!

He watched her unease mount and almost felt sorry for her. She'd made a gross error of judgement; a far greater error than her betrayal three years ago.

By tricking him into coming here, wasting his time when he should be searching for the child in the photograph, she'd just reignited the fire of retribution he'd banked down all this time.

He inhaled an anticipatory breath, absently noting he was no longer as disgruntled by the weather as he'd been minutes ago.

'So, Mia, are you going to invite me in?'

In the tiny region of her mind not frozen in disbelief, Mia absorbed the deep smoothness of Rocco Vitelli's voice, the way its low timbre slid over her senses like warm, sun-kissed honey. But her shock soon dissipated, forcefully wrenched aside by a different set of terrifying emotions.

'You can't be here!'

Throwing her weight behind the door, she fought to slam it shut. It barely moved a few inches before one strong hand held it open, ridiculing her efforts.

'What's the meaning of this?'

His voice, alternately heard in her dreams and nightmares, but always with that smoky, gravelly Italian inflection, caused tiny explosions along her nerve endings.

'I don't know what game you're playing, but you're not getting me into trouble by turning up on my doorstep.'

'Getting you into trouble? Shouldn't that be, "Ciao, Rocco. How have you been?" After all, you orchestrated this meeting.' With lithe grace, he entered, forcing her to abandon the door or risk collision with his hard, lean body.

Her heart hammered as she watched his tall, dark form fill her living room, her sanctuary.

Dear heaven, Rocco was here, in her home.

Tension gripped her throat, but she forced herself to speak. 'I've no idea what you mean. But I want you to get out, Rocco. Mrs Hart, my neighbour, will testify that you turned up on my doorstep unannounced.' Through her window, she spotted his silver limo already attracting attention. Good. If, by some stroke of bad luck, Mrs Hart had vacated her normal window-seat vigil, she'd have other witnesses.

Twin brows the shade of raven's wings shot up. 'Testify? In trouble with the law again, *cara*? What on earth have you got yourself into this time?' He advanced as he spoke, intense dark blue eyes holding her prisoner until he stood close, way too close.

She stood her ground, refusing to retreat. 'What have I got myself into? Is that some sort of joke?'

He moved closer, the gleam in his eyes spiking her nervousness.

'You must be desperate if you're relying on neighbours to bail you out of whatever predicament you're in.' He paused a beat, eyes narrowed. 'Or is that why I'm here?'

His deeply masculine scent hit her nostrils, triggering memories she'd hoped never to recall. 'What do you mean, is that why you're here? This is my house. You've turned up unannounced. I want you to leave. Right now.'

He froze, as if captured in the frame of a lens.

No matter how many times she saw it happen, Rocco's ability to remain completely motionless fascinated her. She stared, much the same way she'd stood behind her son's door, staring, fascinated, less than ten minutes ago—

Gianni.

She closed her eyes. *Breathe, just breathe.*

This is just a nightmare. It'll be over in a few minutes.

'I detest games, *cara*.' Dark menace tinged his voice. 'You've lured me here, the least you can do is tell me why.'

Her eyes snapped open. '*Lured* you here? Are you mad?'

His face darkened. 'On the contrary, my mind has never been clearer. Which member of my staff did you bribe this time to pull this stunt?'

She gasped. 'I beg your pardon?'

'Isn't that your *modus operandi*?' he continued in a low silky tone. 'Using members of my staff to lay your hands on property that's not yours? Who gave you my grandmother's itinerary? Or mine, for that matter? It's not my driver or my pilot. They've both been with me for years. I trust them both implicitly.'

Pain stung through her body. After what he'd put her through, she'd never dreamed she'd see Rocco again. Yet here he was, tall, dark, lethal, in her home, spouting the same accusations, intent on exacting more retribution.

Three years ago, she'd foolishly believed nothing could be worse than having all your wishes granted, only to have them snatched away in the cruellest way possible.

But nothing had compared with what he'd done after he'd ordered her out of his life. When he'd discovered she was daring to contact him, daring to make him change his mind about her, to hear her out. *Then*, the real retribution had been exacted. *Then*, she'd experienced the full might of Rocco Vitelli.

'I've no idea what you're talking about.' The words slipped past lips frozen with renewed pain at how this gorgeous, heartless man had caused her life to implode.

A grim smile curved his lips. 'Still wasting your breath on lies? Why am I surprised? After all, a leopard doesn't change its spots, does it, *cara*? Or are you more of a snake? Either way, a word of advice: next time you try to entice a man, dress appropriately for the occasion. Baggy jeans and a threadbare top aren't a turn-on.'

Hot, sharp anger shot through her. 'How dare you—'

'Save your protests and tell me why I'm really here.'

Tears prickled her eyes and she blinked furiously. 'No, I will not save them. I told you then and I'm telling you now, I never stole from you!'

His lips curled. 'Then explain to me how the blueprints, locked in my safe on an encrypted flash drive, ended up in your possession? Or how the same firm who'd bid against Vitelli Construction ended up with copies of it right after your meeting with them?'

She angled her chin. 'I told you before, I've no idea.'

'And like I told you then, you are a liar.' Heavy scorn laced his words.

She'd imagined herself immune against this intense, searing ache. She was wrong. Renewed pain clenched her heart, squeezed until her breath cracked in her lungs. But damn it, she'd suffered enough. He'd humiliated her, dragged her name and reputation through court, and, worst of all, denied his unborn child. And now he'd turned up for what reason? To rub even more of his twisted brand of justice in her face?

Anger welled higher. 'I don't care what you think. What I want is for you to leave my house.' Thankfully, her voice emerged cold, steady. 'Now.'

Before Gianni woke up. Rocco might not care about his child, but Mia intended to keep the brutal truth of what his father had done to them from her son.

She shot a glance towards the stairs and prayed Gianni hadn't heard the raised voices. Sensing Rocco's incisive gaze on her, she quickly averted her eyes.

'Are you saying you didn't arrange this meeting?' Only his lips moved. The rest of him remained carved in stone.

The question was so ludicrous she would've laughed, had anxiety and the deep shame of unwanted, erotic heat not continued to surge like a rising tide inside her.

'I most certainly did not. If this is some sort of game, I don't appreciate it.' And if she received another intimidating letter from his lawyers, she'd fight it. There had to be grounds against this sort of behaviour. A claim for harassment at the very least.

His gaze narrowed. 'Game? You think I would choose to be anywhere near you?'

The stark disbelief in his tone grated. Loath to let him see the devastation his words caused, she whirled and headed for the farthest seat, which in the small space was only a handful of steps away.

She longed to sink into the armchair that'd been her grandmother's favourite seat, seek comfort from its familiar smell, but that would show weakness.

Instead, she sought refuge behind the chair, her hands gripping the headrest. She was glad for its sturdiness when her eyes settled more firmly on him.

Raw, devastating masculinity. Three years had only added to the gravity of power that surrounded him like an invisible cloak, made all the more distinguished by the faintest sprinkle of grey in his otherwise jet-black hair. His handmade Italian designer suit sat on broad shoulders in perfect symmetry to his well-honed physique.

From stinging, unbidden memory, she knew his six-foot-four frame carried not an ounce of spare flesh. Its sleek, toned muscle, hard planes and smooth contours had once held her fascination for embarrassingly long periods of time.

But it was his face—the arrogant jut of nose, chiselled cheekbones and square jaw sporting a day's stubble—that repeatedly took her breath away. Deep-set blue eyes the colour of a stormy summer night could capture a rapt audience, burn with ferocious passion or freeze with heart-stopping cruelty.

Her gaze dropped to the curved sensuality of his lips and an electrifying sizzle ignited deep in her belly. Dear Lord, what those lips had done to her!

Lifting her gaze, she found him studying her as intensely as she studied him. She needed to get rid of him. Now!

'What you choose to do isn't my concern, Rocco.

What I care about is that you're in my house, without my permission.'

Her grip tightened on the chair when his head cocked slightly. Laser-sharp eyes bored into her and, even from the across the room, their white-hot heat consumed her.

'Are you sure? You can barely breathe from your excitement, yet you expect me to believe that this... reunion wasn't planned?' His disbelief mocked her.

She should've been mortified by how accurately he'd read her. Yet all she felt was a shockingly visceral need; a need that whipped at her with unbelievable force. Swallowing hard, she tried for a careless shrug.

'Don't confuse anger with arousal, Rocco. I've always had my doubts about some of the people you employ. Someone has obviously made a mistake. Again.'

The last word hung between them. He acknowledged it with a cynical smile. 'You too were once my employee. Until you managed to successfully elevate your status.'

'Believe what you want. This—' she waved her hand between them '—wasn't my doing.'

He strolled to her, reached out and ran a long, graceful finger down her heated cheek. 'You were always very good at denial, weren't you, *tesoro*?' His thumb caressed her lower lip, his voice low, hypnotic.

Mia snatched in a fevered breath as delicious flames licked through her. His heated scent wrapped around her like a magician's spell and she fought to remain sane. She couldn't, *wouldn't*, let him drag her back to that dangerous, euphoric place where she'd lost more than just her power of speech. She had more important things to think about.

Like Gianni awakening with Rocco still in the house.

'This conversation is going nowhere. You've obviously taken the wrong turn somewhere. Tell me where you wish to go and I'll happily point you in the right direction.'

He ignored her suggestion and continued his caress along her jaw, sparking a belly-clenching hunger that terrified her.

'You surprise me by maintaining the same tired line of defence. There was an appointment in your electronic diary both on your computer and your phone; a meeting took place during which you discussed confidential plans you were working on at Vitelli Construction. This was corroborated by more than one person.'

He was determined to drag her through their last, humiliating encounter, where he'd hurled soul-searing accusations at her. But short of throwing him out of her house—an impossibility given his sheer size—she had to get through this as quickly as possible.

'I never denied attending that meeting, but I thought I was acting in my capacity as your structural engineer.'

He cupped her chin and tilted her face to his. 'Yet you conveniently neglected to mention you'd passed on sensitive information regarding the Abu Dhabi project. And the fact that you'd accepted a job offer with a company in direct competition with mine.'

Mia gritted her teeth and breathed through her rising stress. 'I didn't divulge sensitive information. And the job was offered. Out of politeness I said I'd think about it. Besides, against Vitelli Construction, they would never have been serious competition.'

A superior smile curved his lips. 'I agree. That aspect of your betrayal was sorely misjudged and didn't cause me even a moment's discomfort.'

She sucked in an astonished breath. If Rocco hadn't condemned her for that... 'Then why—?'

His smile disappeared. The atmosphere turned from darkly sensual to arctic in the space of a heartbeat. 'You dare to ask me *why*?'

Confused, she rubbed her temple. 'Correct me if I'm wrong, but you broke off our engagement, fired me and threw me out of the Milan headquarters because you thought I'd stolen your blueprints and given them to your competitor to secure myself a job.'

'I didn't think. I knew it for a fact.'

'So, if you cared so little about that, what exactly ended our relationship?'

He carried on regarding her, his expression cold, forbidding.

Rocco wasn't a man to be crossed. She knew this from painful experience. So why was she questioning him? Why not keep her mouth shut, let him leave? What did it matter that he'd ended their relationship two months before their wedding? What did it matter that it appeared the subject of the stolen blueprints wasn't the only thing that had blackened her in his eyes?

What he'd done afterwards was unforgivable. He'd ruined her life and dismissed his unborn child with heartless cruelty. Which was why she needed to tread carefully. For Gianni's sake, she couldn't end up in jail—

'Are you serious?' he bit out eventually.

Mia waved him away with fabricated flippancy. 'It doesn't matter—'

'Doesn't matter? Have you any idea what your betrayal did to my grandmother? Do you know the heartache you caused by telling her you had no intention of ever bearing my child?'

She gasped. 'But—'

'She was inconsolable for weeks!'

The ferocity of his tone dried her words.

Rocco's grandmother meant the world to him, which meant she'd become immediately important to Mia. It hadn't been difficult to see why Rocco worshipped the ground his *nonna* walked on. Her instant, unconditional affection had soothed the deep ache caused by the circumstances of her own mother's distance and indifference and the slow decline in her health Mia attributed to her lifelong bitterness and apathy.

'It was never my intention to upset her.'

Rocco inhaled deeply. 'I'll give you one last chance. Tell me why I'm here.'

'Perhaps your hearing is faulty, Rocco. I didn't summon you here. So why don't you tell me why *you are* here,' she tossed back, fighting rising panic.

He didn't answer. After several heartbeats, his gaze left hers to conduct a survey of the shabby clutter of the tiny room.

The furniture had seen better days, but wasn't threadbare. Her grandmother had taken pride in her home, unlike the tiny flat Mia had shared with her mother. *That* home had reeked of apathy, despair and bitterness, and it'd shown in everything from the dark curtains to the cold floors and the callous disregard Mia had endured. All because she'd deigned to be born.

Mia was a little ashamed to admit that, mingled with

the guilt she'd felt at distancing herself from her mother's cold orbit at the first chance she got by taking a job first in London, and then in Italy, had been a tinge of relief.

But with every dispiriting visit and phone call in those intervening years before ill health had claimed her mother, Mia had been plagued with doubt as to her own worthiness. As to whether she would visit the same indifference and apathy on her future offspring.

It was why she'd been terrified of motherhood. Why she'd refused to even contemplate such a sacred and lifelong undertaking. How could she? When she had no clue what maternal love was? When she had no way of ascertaining whether her mother's bitterness had rubbed off on her and risked being transferred to her own child?

Of course, she'd had her answer the moment Gianni was placed in her arms.

Gianni.

Thoughts of her son grounded her in the present.

She watched Rocco inspect her house.

She'd taken down the framed pictures and boxed them away so she could repair the peeling paint, but her dwindling finances had stalled that project. Cheap rugs provided relief from the cold hardwood floors and a place for Gianni to play in front of the grated fire when the weather was too cold.

It took seconds for Rocco to take this all in, for his gaze to snap back to trap hers.

'You need money, *si*? Judging from the state of this place, you're short on cash.' His head snapped up. 'Are you sick?'

'No.'

Suspicion narrowing his eyes, he nudged a finger under her chin. 'But you need cash?'

Of course she needed cash. Thanks to his effective blacklisting, she'd been forced to give up her much-cherished career. Any other means of earning a living while caring for Gianni was virtually non-existent and the last of her savings was almost gone. But she'd crawl on hot coals to hell before she admitted it to the man responsible for ripping her life apart.

Her hands tightened on the chair. 'I need nothing from you. Except for you to leave my house.' Before she did the unthinkable, like give in to the need to touch him.

Go. Please, just go.

Finally, he dropped his hand. She immediately berated herself for wishing it back.

'I'm beginning to think this has been an…unfortunate mistake.'

She exhaled in relief. 'Can I trust that it won't happen again?' As long as there were no repercussions, she would be grateful.

Icy disdain tightened his face as he turned away. 'I dismissed you from my life long ago. Believe that I've no wish to set eyes on you again.'

'Trust me, I feel the same.' Her voice emerged with a calm she didn't feel. Inside, she wanted to scream. She clamped her mouth together as tears threatened, stung into being by his harsh words.

Blinking furiously, she watched him leave from behind the solid safety of her chair, even now unable to stop herself from feasting hungry eyes on his broad back, recalling the warmth of his skin under her searching caress, the silky luxury of his hair she'd once loved to run her fingers through.

He paused at the door. 'I don't know who orchestrated this meeting, but I will get to the bottom of this incident. And whoever is responsible will pay.'

She managed a stiff smile, her muscles threatening to seize up from the rigid control she kept on them. 'You still haven't told me *why* you came here in the first place, but, since I'm not responsible, I don't much care. Goodbye, Rocco.'

She didn't move until the door shut behind him. Then, galvanised by sheer self-preservation, she rushed to the window to make sure he was really leaving.

His long limbs had already carried him to his car by the time she nudged aside the curtain.

Inexplicable longing battered her. Her heartbeat thundered as she acknowledged that this might be the last time she ever saw Rocco Vitelli.

Greedily, she drank him in: the way his hair lifted in the cold breeze, the set of his strong, powerful shoulders as he hunched deeper into his jacket, even the hand he lifted to wave the driver away from opening his door caused her heartbeat to escalate until Mia feared it would burst out of her chest.

Dry-mouthed, she forced herself to turn away. Limbs shaking, she collapsed into the chair and buried her face in her hands, the reality of her lucky escape washing over her.

After several minutes of taking deep, careful breaths, she rose. A strong cup of tea would help get over the shock. That was all it was, she stressed to herself. Seeing Rocco again had shocked her.

Shocked and *excited* her. Reminded her how good they'd been together. In the boardroom. In bed. She closed her eyes in shame, sternly reminding herself of the consequences she'd suffered for once being a lust-sick fool. A stupid, besotted fool.

But she was over that. God, was she over it.

Nothing ripped off rose-tinted glasses quicker than finding out the man you loved saw you only as a brood mare. And a thief.

Realising she was standing in the middle of the room, wringing her hands, she abruptly stilled the movement. She would not let him affect her like this. Whatever ill wind had blown him here, he was gone.

Whirling, she started for the kitchen, then paused.

Something was wrong. With a start, she realised she hadn't heard Rocco's car leave.

The tiny cottage she'd inherited from her grandmother after her passing last year was on the outskirts of a Hampshire village. It was where she'd retreated to after barely surviving the tornado that was Rocco. It was located in a quiet cul-de-sac and at this time of day, before children returned from school, the place was so peaceful, she could normally hear even the quietest engine idling.

Dread crawling up her spine, she moved with leaden feet towards the window and nudged aside her curtain.

Rocco stood on the pavement, deep in conversation with Mrs Hart.

Mia's heart slammed in her chest, then jumped into her throat when Rocco's head jerked up.

No!

His gaze snapped to the window, snagging hers with

the accuracy of a grappling hook. Even from that distance, the look in his eyes knocked the air from her lungs. Fingers frozen around a clump of curtain, she watched in dread as, without breaking eye contact, he retraced his steps down her flagstone path.

This time there was no knock.

He merely turned the handle and strode in. Straight to where she stood. Long, strong fingers pried the curtain from her hand, edged her away from the window.

He reached into his breast pocket.

Her palms grew damp with the rush of apprehension. 'No!' Dear God, not another ghastly letter. What would it demand of her this time? The very heart beating in her chest?

But what he extracted wasn't a letter. It was far too small, barely three inches wide, coloured and glossy.

Bewildered, she watched him pass a thumb over its surface, his gaze fixed on the image. His face was ashen, harsh pants rushing through his clenched teeth as he fought for breath.

Finally, his intense, almost unholy gaze speared hers.

'You wanted to know why I came here? Because Nonna is convinced there is a vital secret I need to uncover. Something that belongs to me. So I'm going to ask you once, Mia. Who is this child? Where is he and, more importantly, *what is he to me*?'

CHAPTER TWO

MIA REELED AS her heart kicked.

Was this some sort of sick, twisted new game? Was Rocco now colluding to make her appear unstable so he could take Gianni away from her?

Over my dead body!

She would go through every legal channel, sell every last possession she owned to pay for lawyers before she let that happen.

'Mia.' Her name, like his statement, was delivered with such care, such precision, that a cold slice of fear knifed through her thoughts.

'Are you serious?' she tossed back.

Rocco took a step forward, until there was less than a foot between them. She craned her neck to stare into his face and almost wished she hadn't.

This close to him, she could see every magnificent masculine feature, breathe in the scent of skin and cologne that was all Rocco, feel it attack her flailing senses from all sides. His eyes, cold, direct and hypnotising, blunted every last weapon she intended to use against him.

One long-fingered hand gripped her chin and Mia was again lost.

Three long years she'd dreamed of his touch. Against her will, in the cold of winter, the long, hot, lazy summer night, she'd yearned for these same fingers that had caressed her to ecstasy, touched her, teased her, made her cry out to join her soul with this man.

And now he was touching her again and she could hardly remain still for the surge of excitement that fizzed through her veins. She wanted to lean into his touch, press his fingers more deeply against her, imprint his skin on hers until she didn't know where he ended and she began.

'Answer me, Mia. Do you know this child?'

Mia jerked away, stung and ashamed.

What was she doing playing right into the hands of her enemy? Rocco no longer had sexual power over her, so why was she standing there, gazing up at him like…like…?

She took a hasty step back, tried to remain calm as her gaze dropped to the picture. A cherubic face smiled back at her with cheeky impertinence. The child's dark blue eyes twinkled with mirth and the mop of black curls danced in a slight breeze. She wanted to reach out and caress the slightly dimpled chin, which some day would deepen like his father's.

Did she know this child?

Of course she knew him.

She'd carried him in her womb for nine months, loved him with every fibre of her being long before he'd delivered the first of many vicious kicks inside her, and adored every strand of hair, every soft velvety inch of him from the moment he was placed in her arms.

'Of course I know him,' she replied, her voice strong and steady with the power of emotion she felt for her son.

Shock detonated in Rocco's eyes.

For a moment there, she'd almost given into the urge to deny knowledge of her own son to keep him safe. After all, Rocco had never met him, so he didn't know what Gianni looked like.

But her innate honesty and fierce pride as Gianni's mother had overridden that urge immediately. Besides, from the look in his eyes, Rocco had expected her to lie. After all, she was an expert at it, right? Well, wrong.

Gianni was her son, and she would do *anything* to protect him.

Rocco's already ashen pallor—from whatever Mrs Hart had said to him—faded even more. Intrigued, she watched the picture waver as his hand trembled.

That in itself was so shocking, so out of character, her eyes flew to his. Rocco? Tremble? Never. Even in bed, in the throes of ecstasy, he'd trumpeted his dominance, much like a lion roaring in triumph.

'And how, exactly, do you know the child?' His voice tremored, his accent thickening on the hoarse whisper.

She gulped, tried to calm the near hysterical warning voice shrieking in her head—*he's playing games with you. Stop him at all costs.* 'You know very well how I know him. And stop calling him *the child.* His name is Gianni.'

He absorbed that with another round of jaw-gritting. 'How do you know him, Mia?'

'I don't appreciate whatever game you're playing, Rocco. Get out of my house. Right now, or I'll call the pol—'

He whirled away from her, clawing visibly trembling fingers through his hair. The action killed off her words long before he reversed direction, closed the gap between them and gripped her arms.

Desperately, she tried to wrest herself from his hold, to curb the sensation stealing through her senses, but he held her easily. And the sorry thing was, Mia didn't really want to fight the torrid sensation cascading through her. The intoxicating memory of how it'd felt to be held like this by Rocco.

'You will tell me what I want to know. Now.' Eyes as dark as a stormy sea threatened to flay her.

The command spurred her to do something other than languish in painful memories. 'No. Go to hell. I will not indulge in this stupid game with you.'

'According to Mrs Hart, he's asleep. His afternoon nap, am I right? Perhaps you'd like me to wait for him to wake? See for myself what you're hiding from me?'

The blood drained from her face. Rocco hadn't changed. If anything, the laser-sharp intellect that had seen him rise from a renowned architect to iconic innovator had been honed even sharper. With a few words, he'd whittled away her resistance.

'No, I think not,' he emphasised with calm incisiveness. 'Instead, you'll answer my question.'

'Why should I?' she croaked through lips tingling with a thousand firing nerves.

'Because I dropped everything to come here to find out and I will not be toyed with.'

Her fists slammed against his chest as anger fired up within her. 'Yet you're happy to do the same with other people? Does it give you a sick thrill to hold the power of life and death in your hands, Rocco?'

His lips twisted. 'You've developed quite a taste for melodrama since we last met, *cara*. But it's a taste I don't have the time or inclination to indulge in.'

She shivered at his chilling tone. 'Why now, Rocco? Do you have some sadistic urge to see how I live? See what you've reduced me to?'

He started to frown but she waved him away.

'Don't bother pretending. Thing is, I never took you for a sadist. More fool me, right? Because when it comes down to it, what had I really known about the man I was once engaged to marry?' Nothing because, in the end, the man she'd loved, the man who'd purportedly respected her intellect and creativity by day and whispered heated, magical promises to her as he'd worshipped her body with his own by night, had morphed into a snarling, heartless, vitriol-spewing monster.

A monster who was now asking her a question to which he already knew the answer!

He dropped his arms and paced the living room once more, his expression bewildered. The action focused her gaze on his stunning, harsh beauty. Unforgiving blue eyes glowered at her, giving her no quarter from their lethal demand. Cheekbones seemingly fashioned from polished marble stood out in haughty relief; his dark stubbled jaw made her fingers tingle wildly.

'You're talking in riddles and my patience is running thin, Mia.'

She could verify that from the frantic pulse throbbing in his temple. 'Then you can leave the same way you came. The door is still open.'

Use it. Please, please leave.

'*Christo!* Answer me!' he barked.

'Why?'

He growled and uttered a single curse. It was a curse she'd heard him utter only once before, when it had seemed her begging and grovelling for a chance to explain had got too much for him to stomach three years ago. Then, he'd thrust her away from him and marched out, telling her in no uncertain terms that she had twenty minutes to pack her bags and clear out of his Palermo villa before his security detail gave her a firm hand.

Now those hands were braced on his hips, his eyes narrowed on her face. She forced herself not to cower as she witnessed his failing patience in the hectic colour slashing his contoured cheekbones.

Lifting her head, she glared right back. 'You know exactly who he is, Rocco. What I don't know is why you're pretending otherwise. You know Gianni's my son. Just as you know he's yours!'

Silence, thick and monumental, circled them, rising, whipping up her bewilderment until it threatened to choke her.

Rocco's hands dropped to his sides in shock. Then he *trembled*. She had to hand it to him. His acting skills were impeccable. Oscar-worthy.

'*You lie.*' His voice was a strangled rasp, barely audible over her thundering heart. 'You lie,' he insisted, his voice growing deadlier with each word.

His skin was stretched taut over frozen features and his eyes—although they bored into hers—held the stunned glaze of disbelief and made her think he wasn't really seeing her.

'For goodness' sake. Why would I lie about something like this?' Something he already knew.

Her answer seemed to rouse him from some dark, unknown place. He focused on her, and the look in the stormy depths stilled her breath.

'This child is mine?'

Again the warning shrieked in her head. Rocco Vitelli was playing a very dangerous game with her; a game she had no way of winning unless she focused. To do that she needed to get away from him, put some space between herself and his heady, mind-altering proximity.

She took a step out of his immediate orbit. He didn't follow. Because he was too stunned?

Certainly the way his eyes had darkened, the way his hand wasn't quite steady when he raked through his dark hair again, implied he was.

But…why? He'd known about his child as soon as she'd found out she was pregnant with Gianni. And she'd kept him apprised of every single milestone in her early pregnancy in the hope that he'd come around, that he'd let her explain—again—her version of the events that had ended their engagement. Of course, in the end, that had backfired on her big time. Her life had been hurled into a hellish nightmare the likes of which she could never have imagined.

Rocco had seen to that.

Rocco, the same man who now stood before her, feigning aggrieved innocence.

She backed towards the door. With any luck, Mrs Hart would still be lurking outside, greedy for gossip. This time Mia didn't mind who saw her. She'd need witnesses who'd testify that she hadn't invited Rocco here. Mrs Hart would be perfect—

'I want to see him.'

The simple, hoarse words stopped her in her tracks.

She whirled to face him. 'No. What you need to do is leave my house.'

'You tell me I have a son, sleeping upstairs, a child I have never seen, and you expect me to leave?' His accent was even thicker, his voice rising with incredulity.

The injustice of the accusation stung deep. She abandoned her plan to seek witnesses and stalked back to him. 'And whose fault is that, Rocco? You had endless chances and chose not to take them. So don't you dare act as if any of this is my fault.'

'Not your fault? Who should I blame, then, *cara*, hmm?' The vibrant olive tinge to his skin hadn't quite returned, but his eyes were alive again, threatening to tear chunks out of her with each glance.

'I know it's very hard for you, but perhaps you could try pointing the finger at yourself? Instead of getting to know him, of taking the chance to be a part of your son's life, to watch him grow, you decided to punish an innocent child instead.' Her voice threatened to crack, but she swallowed away the pain. 'Well, you'll see him over my dead body!'

'*Maledizione!* From the melodramatic, you've now descended into the downright absurd. Punish an innocent child? If by that you mean depriving him of his right to know his father, then you should be pointing the finger at yourself. *Dio mio*, you sound delusional!'

Neon lights lit up in her head as her worst fears were confirmed. 'Finally. I was wondering when you'd get round to making that accusation. You've changed, Rocco. You used to get to the point pretty much instantly. Now you go around the houses, and what for? Playing the puppet master is now your thing, is it?'

'*Che?* What in heaven's name are you talking about?' He shook his head, reached out and grasped her wrist. 'Something's not right with you. Since I got here, nothing you've said has made any sense.'

Mia couldn't stop the hysterical laughter that bubbled up in her throat or the cheap thrill it gave her when Rocco's frown intensified. Her laughter grew until warm tears streamed down her cheeks. 'You…you are really priceless, Rocco, you know that?'

His jaw tightened. 'Enough! I've had more than enough of your histrionics. I want to see the child, and I want to see him now.'

That dissolved the laughter instantly. Somewhere in her mind, she registered he still hadn't used Gianni's name, almost as if her son wasn't real to him. But if Rocco didn't want to acknowledge their child, why was he insisting on seeing him?

'Not until you tell me why. Why do you want to see him, Rocco? Why now?'

Rocco tried his damnedest to stop his senses spinning. To still for a moment so he could formulate one clear, coherent thought.

But the moment he focused on Mia, on the feisty woman whose pulse hammered beneath his hand, everything began to blur again.

Mia.

His child.

Here. Living in this sleepy village in the middle of Nowhere, England.

Mia, spouting some garbage about him ignoring his child, not taking the chance to know his own flesh and blood. The blur intensified, threatening to spin out of control. A door cracked open in his mind, throwing more light on the long-buried yearning he'd sealed drum-tight. Dreams of a family, of love, hope, everything that had callously been denied him, until Nonna had taken control, sacrificed everything for her grandson, shown him a different way, not knowing the scars were already too deep to heal—

He slammed the door shut, gritted his teeth and forced himself to focus.

How could Mia believe that he'd ignore his child's existence? When he'd made no secret of how much he'd wanted an heir. A fact she'd known but had had no intention of fulfilling with him when she'd rapturously accepted his proposal...

From what the neighbour had said, the child looked healthy and seemed well taken care of. *Seemed*. But who knew what went on behind closed doors?

Madre di Dio! He couldn't believe Nonna had been right. The sheer, fragile coincidence, the flimsiness of fate, of what he could've missed all his life, terrified him to his very soul. Made him want to curse. And punish.

What if his grandmother had taken another route to mass? What if she hadn't been paying attention to the electronic billboard on the side of the road?

The thought that he could've remained oblivious to his son's existence, his own flesh and blood, sent a renewed wave of anguish and anger through him. And all because of the selfishness of the woman in front of him.

What had she asked him? Why now?

As if he'd ever been given the chance before. He took a calming breath, stifling the urge to deliver a tiny dose of what he was going through.

As an only child, he had been so desperately lonely, what with his parents' callous and blatant neglect, and Nonna working all hours to provide for him. At the age of ten, watching his grandmother scrimp and save to make ends meet, he'd vowed first to make enough money to see her in luxury in her old age, a vow he'd made come true hundreds of millions of times over. His second vow had been that no child of his—should he ever have them—would grow up experiencing the deep scars of neglect and cruel indifference. For Nonna's sake, he'd never ruled out marriage. But to do that he'd also vowed to find a suitable wife who would fulfil his strict parameters of care for his future children.

That particular goal had been elusive, and over the years it'd slowly eroded until he'd eventually given up any hope of ever fulfilling it.

Then he'd met Mia Gallagher. With her, he'd contemplated the rebirth of all his long-cherished but slowly abandoned goals. Or so he'd thought.

She'd led him on with promises of a future he'd all but encouraged Nonna to give up on. Right up to the weeks before he'd placed his wedding ring on her finger. Then he'd had the scales pulled viciously from his eyes.

Her lies he could tolerate, if not forgive. But this! Keeping his own flesh and blood from him?

'Are you insane to ask me why I want to know the existence of my own child? You think anything will come between me and my flesh and blood?' The ugly sneer he heard in his own voice made his anger rise. He never lost control like this. Never. But this woman had driven him to the very brink of sanity. Once three years ago. And now.

Her eyes had widened. Clear green eyes he'd once upon a time drowned in; eyes he'd seen fill with tears when he'd gone down on one knee in the presence of his beloved grandmother and proposed to her; eyes he'd watched darken in passion as she'd whispered how much she adored him, how he meant everything to her, how much she couldn't wait to join her life with his.

Of course, she'd had a different interpretation of just what she'd been hoping for from their union.

Clear, luminous, almond-shaped *deceptive* eyes. Eyes that held his without a hint of remorse even in the face of her barefaced lies. Add that slight tremble to her plump, kissable lips and any man was destined to believe every insincere word she uttered.

Any man but him. He'd taken her measure when she'd lied through her teeth even in the face of concrete evidence three years ago.

So why was he standing here, trying to reason with her? Could he even believe the child was his? Well, only one way to find out. He whirled away from her and stalked to the stairs. A house this small, it wouldn't be difficult to find the child.

An affronted gasp sounded behind him as she scrambled after him.

'Wait! Where do you think you're going?'

Good, that was the reaction he wanted. Maybe now she'd drop this crazy pretence and take him seriously.

His foot was on the second step when her small hands closed over his bicep. The kick of lust he'd felt earlier returned, sharper, deeper, awakening senses he'd thought long dead. His anger only escalated and he stiffened against the reaction, ready to pull away.

'Rocco, wait! You can't go up there!'

He glanced down into her heart-shaped face and read real terror there. *Dio!* Did she think he intended to harm the child?

Or was she reacting to something else? He stepped down quicker than he'd climbed.

'Why are you so afraid to let me see him? Is he unwell? Is that why you've kept me in the dark about his existence? If so, know that nothing will—'

She jerked back with a frown. 'No, of course not. Gianni is a perfectly happy and healthy little boy,' she defended hotly.

Rocco let out the breath locked in his lungs and regained the step. '*Bene*, then nothing should prevent me from seeing him. Do you want to lead the way, or should I just wander from room to room until I find him?'

Stormy eyes snapped with dislike. 'I'd prefer neither option, quite frankly.'

He shrugged, then felt a mild sense of loss when the movement dislodged her hands. 'Fine. Stay here.' One way or the other he intended to see the child—*his son*. He'd already been denied his existence for over over two years.

Dio, two years! He forced himself to calm down and took the stairs three at a time. She scrambled up after him, but his eyes were glued to the door at the top of the stairs.

Was that where his son slept? A hot rush of air filled his lungs, leaving him faint by the time he reached the last step. Would there be an instant, instinctive bond, or would he, thanks to the actions of the slip of a woman behind him, have to get to know his own flesh and blood?

Rocco's heart hammered the way it never had before as he faced the door. Reaching out, he grasped the doorknob.

'That's not Gianni's room,' Mia's husky voice said from behind him.

He jerked back with a mixture of relief and trepidation. For in that instant, before his hand had closed over the knob, he'd felt as if, somehow, he'd failed his son. That by cutting Mia off so completely, maybe he'd somehow been to blame for not knowing of his son's existence.

Which was ridiculous, he reminded himself. He'd done nothing wrong. He'd thrown Mia out of his life because she'd turned out to be a thief and a liar. And while he wouldn't have chosen such a person as the mother of his child, the situation was what it was. But if the child behind the next door was his, a fact an unknown instinct was warning him was so, he would move heaven and earth to make up for the time he'd lost. Taking a deep, restorative breath, he faced her. One look at his face, and she moved swiftly along the short corridor.

She stopped in front of a door painted a bright yellow. Stencils of racing cars and teddy bears danced on the frame and a brightly coloured sign proclaimed it as Gianni's Kingdom. The smile that tugged at the corner of his mouth was quickly suppressed beneath the torrent of emotion raging through him.

With a beseeching look at him, Mia slowly opened the door and tiptoed in.

Rocco stood on the threshold, knowing without a shadow of a doubt his life was about to change for ever. But he couldn't have turned back if his life depended on it.

He stepped into the room. The curtains, stencilled with another racing-car theme, were drawn against the afternoon sun, so at first he couldn't see the small lump burrowed underneath a brightly coloured blanket.

Another step brought him closer to the cot.

A tremor went through him at his first glimpse of his son.

Dark curls peeked out from the top of the blanket. Even that small sight had the power to stop Rocco's breath. As he watched, the boy stretched in his sleep, a slow, indulgent movement that revealed the full impact of his perfect, innocent, heart-stoppingly beautiful face. A face that marked him, without a shadow of a doubt, as a Vitelli.

A face that Rocco knew he would treasure for ever.

CHAPTER THREE

FOR THE SECOND time in the space of an hour, Mia watched, fascinated, as Rocco Vitelli froze into absolute stillness. Were it not for the pulse that raced in his neck, she would've believed he'd turned into one of the polished marble statues of his beloved Palermo.

Haltingly, she took another step closer and cast a frantic glance at him. His eyes were on Gianni, the feverish blue fastened with staggering intensity on her son.

Their son.

Gianni was lost in the land of slumber, the effects of swimming and running around in the park having taken their toll. Her gaze returned to Rocco and the resemblance between father and son hit her dead in the chest. Not having seen them this close before, she'd had no warning how strong the likeness was between them. Confronted with it now, there was no doubt.

Gianni had the beginnings of the strong Vitelli jaw, the dark slashed eyebrows and high cheekbones of his antecedents.

Beside her, Rocco drew in a shuddering breath. Slowly, his fist unclenched and reached towards his son. Long, strong fingers caressed one plump curl, which immediately clung into his touch. With trance-like movements, he sank down until his face was almost level with Gianni's through the slats in his cot.

'Mio figlio,' he breathed. My son.

Without warning, Gianni's eyes popped open.

Father and son stared at each other for one heart-stopping moment.

Mia forgot to breathe. Her nails dug into her fingers as her limbs froze.

Then just as abruptly, Gianni blinked, rolled onto his side and promptly went back to sleep.

Mia's breath shuddered out as Rocco surged to his feet. He seemed to have trouble breathing. He swallowed several times, his eyes still fixed on their sleeping son.

Then, utterly awestruck, her heart leaping into her throat, she watched a single tear roll down his cheek. With a shaky hand, he brushed it off his face. His massive shoulders heaved as he inhaled. Her own eyes prickled, and she bit her lip to stop the distressed sound in her throat from emerging. Before she could utter a word, he stepped back from the cot.

When he turned to face her, his face was clenched tight, but his eyes were ablaze with turbulent emotion.

'Downstairs. Now, *per favore*,' he bit out.

Without looking back at his son, Rocco left the room.

Mia took her time, composing herself while slowly tucking the blanket more securely around her son.

Downstairs, she found him once again pacing her living room in tight, tension-filled circles.

She wanted him out, as quickly as possible. But after

what she'd witnessed upstairs, she wasn't so sure she could accuse him of playing games any longer. It was the same instinct that warned her not to break the silence. So she stood, one hand braced against the banister.

Eventually he stopped in front of the box on the floor, his eyes zeroing in on its contents. Bending his large frame, he plucked up a picture of Gianni, taken moments after his birth. He stared at it for endless moments. Then he brushed the surface with his thumb, much the same way he'd done with the picture in his pocket.

When his gaze snagged hers, it held a mixture of stark bleakness and eviscerating anger that had her clutching the banister tighter. 'Gianni's my son. You kept him from me. Why?'

The raw pain cracking his voice rendered Mia speechless as the depth of his anguish rocked her soul.

She opened her mouth but no words emerged.

He held out one hand to her in entreaty, further confounding her. '*Per favore*, tell me why,' he muttered in a ragged whisper.

Mia dragged in a desperate, bewildered breath. 'I didn't keep him from you, Rocco. You know I didn't. I—'

His hand slashed through the air. 'You keep insisting that I did. But I didn't know, Mia. I didn't know!' he roared.

'How on earth can you say that? How can you insist on calling me a liar at every turn but then tell me you didn't know you had a child? What's *really* going on, Rocco? You claim you weren't aware of Gianni's existence, so how come you have his picture and my address?'

She reeled as another bolt of pain slashed across his face.

'Nonna saw his picture on a billboard on the way to mass yesterday morning. According to her companion, she took one look at the picture and became so agitated she almost collapsed. My staff thought she'd lost her mind when she insisted the boy in the picture was my child. The doctor was called. She was so distressed she had to be sedated. But eventually, when she'd calmed enough, she called me, told me I had a son and I had to find him.'

Mia gasped. 'But how…how was she so sure?'

'There's a picture of me, almost identical to this one. Nonna wears it in the locket around her neck. It was the only proof she had that she hadn't lost her mind. Hell, even I didn't believe it at first. But she was adamant, almost to the point of hysteria, that I dropped everything and flew back from Abu Dhabi to see her.'

A memory resurfaced. 'I know that picture. She showed it to me once, but when she said it was of her *bambino*, I assumed it was your father. That was you?'

He gave a stiff nod.

'And so she called you, based on seeing Gianni's picture on a billboard?'

'*Sì.*' His hand clenched over the picture and swallowed hard before he looked up. 'And to think I almost dismissed her pleas. For as long as I live, I will owe her a priceless debt for insisting I come here. If she hadn't, I would still be in the dark about my son's existence.' He speared her with a look so unnerving, Mia's stomach twisted into thick knots. He tucked the picture away. 'Later, we will address the subject of why my son is posing in a children's catalogue. For now, I'm still waiting for an explanation.'

Mia's head throbbed from absorbing the information pelting her like icy rocks in a hailstorm. She wanted to let go of the banister, but she wasn't sure her legs would support her if she did. Rocco gave no quarter. He stood, hands on hips, tall and solid in front of her, waiting for answers.

But they were answers she knew he already had. There was no way he could not have known about Gianni. Hell, she still had the last letter from his lawyers cautioning her against asking for child support.

Confusion mingled with all the other emotions welling up inside her and she massaged her nape in the vain hope of easing her tense muscles and helping her think clearly. 'Help me out here, because I'm really confused. Did you have an accident recently? Or bump your head and develop amnesia? Because—'

His face darkened even further and with a frustrated growl he dropped the picture back in the box.

'Sorry, I had to ask. Because that would be the only reason why you would be asking me these questions.'

'Santa cielo!' He closed his eyes, took a calming breath, then spiked his fingers through his dark hair, ruffling the normally neat strands into further disarray. 'Fine. Let's just pretend I've been in an accident recently; that I have no memory of the last three years. What would've happened that I'd need to know?'

She licked dry lips and swallowed. 'Besides showing up here after making my life a living hell for three years, and then pretending you don't know anything about it? Well, for starters, you should know to be ashamed of yourself, but then you have no shame, do you? You only see things in black and white, with no tolerance for grey. You decided I was guilty of stealing and condemned me to pay for the rest of my life. My God, even if by some stretch of the imagination I would've been willing to forgive you for that, what you've done to my son I find very difficult to forgive and I will never forgive you for that, Rocco. Never—'

She was too busy venting long-suppressed emotions and shaking so hard with the pain that came with it that she didn't see him approach, didn't sense the danger signs until it was too late. Too late to stop him from grabbing her; from hauling her hard against his solid frame. To avert her head to avoid the emotional devastation of his lips as they seized hers, ground into hers, forced her shocked lips open to delve into her unguarded mouth. Her stunned senses grappled to find reason, to latch onto her fast-dwindling sanity, but the battle was lost under the attack of a deep, dark resurging hunger.

The hands she braced against his chest to push him away swiftly lost their fight as his tongue took control of hers. That first, singeing assault made her knees buckle. She would've landed in an ungainly heap had it not been for the strong arm around her waist. Within seconds, her hands were curling into his hair, renewing their acquaintance with the sleek short strands. She caressed his nape, his rough, stubbled jaw, the strong curve of his cheek as he continued to wreak havoc on her senses. Pleasure, potent and exquisite, flooded her veins, searing a demanding path straight to that secret, forgotten place between her legs.

In a split second, the direction of his intention changed. Instead of overpowering, he caressed, in place of forceful demand, his hand gentled as he moulded her to his rigid length. And that only sucked her deeper into the maelstrom of feeling this man always evoked within her.

His hand moved lower, brought her even closer to his body. Her gasp as she felt the force of his arousal was swallowed into the heat of their kiss. She groaned deep in her throat, wanting the feeling never to end. When he broke the kiss and moved to her neck, she closed her eyes and threw back her head to give him easy access.

His hard chuckle as his hot mouth teased her pulse made her melt inside. She gave up and shuddered against him as lust-filled gooseflesh raced over her skin. His chuckle turned into deep-throated laughter.

'Your neck is still as sensitive as ever, *cara mia*. It pleases me to know that at least hasn't changed.'

Heat was instantly replaced by cold, cold ice. Dear God, had she lost her mind? She tried to wrench away. 'Damn you! Let me go!'

His grip loosened but he didn't raise his head from the exploration of her neck. In fact, he intensified his attack by passing a lazy tongue over her flesh before nipping it gently between his teeth. 'Why?' he rasped. 'So you can spout more mystifying garbage? No. This is so much better.' Raising his head, he conducted a searing survey over her face, down her neck, to her breasts.

Following his gaze, she saw her nipples had stiffened to painful attention beneath her thin sweater. Heat flamed up her face as he dipped his head and circled one damp tongue over the jersey-covered flesh. Mia was unable to stop the helpless jerk of her body. With a mocking smile, Rocco closed his mouth over his prize, teased the sensitive nub between his teeth until she gave a strangled cry. 'Indeed, I prefer to use the language of lust. At least our bodies don't lie, even after all these years.' Straightening up, he backed her against the banister, then moved closer still, imprinting the hard, lean tower of masculinity against her.

Fire threatened to melt the ice she'd fought hard to build around her emotions, even as she acknowledged that, when it came to Rocco, that task was an uphill battle. But she couldn't afford to let him do this to her. It was humiliating enough that she'd let herself drown in his kiss. Surrendering to his touch a second time was unthinkable. Especially given the devastation he'd wreaked on her life.

'Well, this body wants you as far from hers as possible,' she informed him coldly.

His lips twisted in a parody of a smile. 'Really? Then why does it curve around mine? Why are your arms clamped around my neck? Your hips undulating against mine with an urgent need for me to take you, right here, right now?' he asked huskily.

The heat that flooded up her face only made the scarlet haze rise again. 'I swear on everything I hold dear, if you call me a liar one more time, you'll regret it.'

'Since screaming and frightening my son is out of the question, and the phone is on the other side of the room, I'm curious to see what else you come up with.'

'For starters, my knee, between your legs. Would that get your attention?'

He let out a short bark of laughter. 'I'll give you some free advice, *amante*. Never let your opponent know your intention before you act,' he told her. But he made no move to protect himself.

And it galled her that he knew she wouldn't follow through; that when it came to the two of them, the only act that bordered on turbulent was the insane passion that threatened to rage out of control.

But she had to do something. She would surely lose her mind trapped against him like this, the heat of his body flaming hers; the thick ride of his erection nestling so forcefully against her belly, reminding her with searing accuracy how it had felt to have that power, that delirium-inducing force inside her.

With increasing desperation, she threw caution to the wind.

'Let me go. Or this time I will scream, and I don't care if Gianni wakes up. Maybe it's time he met his monster of a father.'

Her reckless accusation removed every last vestige of laughter from his face. His features tightened into a dark, taut mask and he stilled. But this time she knew he hadn't turned to marble, because she felt the thunder-strong beat of his heart kick up against her breast, felt the harsh exhalation of his breath against her face. And the arm he still held around her waist tightened.

'Clarify that statement, if you please,' he demanded in a deceptively soft tone. 'Why would my son perceive me as a monster?'

Dropping her hands from his nape, she pushed hard

against his chest, but he didn't budge. He merely waited out her feeble efforts until she was panting with frustration. When her gaze clashed with his, he raised one haughty eyebrow.

'Damn you! Because you accused his mother of stalking you! You dragged her into court when she was three months pregnant, exhibited every phone message, every email, every letter she'd sent you, even photographs you'd secretly taken of her as she waited for you in your office. You admitted everything as evidence of her stalking and then convinced the judge to slap a restraining order on her. You didn't even turn up in court because your lawyers informed the judge you were in fear of your life from your unborn child's mother and insisted she was to stay at least five hundred feet from you at all times.' She stabbed a finger in his shoulder. 'Gianni should know that, because of you, his mother hasn't been able to work to provide for him, that all her friends and so-called colleagues would have nothing to do with her when she was branded the pregnant psycho stalker of the great Rocco Vitelli!'

Rocco let her go so abruptly, she stumbled wildly. The sturdy banister was once again her saviour when she fell against it. Chest heaving and struggling not to cry, she turned away from him and collapsed onto the last step.

Damn him.

Damn Rocco Vitelli to hell and back. Reliving her trauma of three years ago was the last thing she wanted to do, but, being who he was, Rocco had pushed and pushed until she'd broken, just as he'd done the last time.

Shame flooded her as she recalled how she'd begged

and pleaded for him to take her back. For one month, she'd rung him every day, emailed him over a dozen times and in the end resorted to letters, which she'd pleaded with one staff member in his mail room to hand-deliver.

The messenger had assured her he'd delivered it, and she knew Rocco had received it because that last letter, where she'd begged him to take her back for the sake of their unborn child, had been one of the letters exhibited at the dreadful hearing. It had been read out loud in court, earning her a pity-filled look from the judge. But it hadn't stopped him from issuing the restraining order, banning her from ever contacting Rocco Vitelli, in person or via electronic channels, before strongly advising her to seek help for her *obsessive* condition.

She'd staggered from the courtroom, dazed, from the ashes her life had turned into seemingly overnight. She'd lost her temp job almost immediately and found out very soon that all other employment avenues were closed to her, the Vitelli name an iron-clad guarantee to overpower the name of Gallagher.

Thank God for her grandmother's unquestioning support when Mia had turned up on her doorstep, pregnant and broken.

Her painful introspection ceased when she opened her eyes and encountered designer-styled shoes planted in front of her. She looked up and up into Rocco's stony face. The grey pallor was back, tingeing his skin and making his eyes look gaunt. His mouth was set in a flat, immoveable line as his hands balled into fists at his sides.

'You have levelled one absurd accusation after another since I walked through this door today, Mia, but this…' he shook his head in stunned disbelief '…this outshines them all.' He retreated to the far end of the room, his broad shoulders stiff, as if trying to keep a tight rein on his control.

'I know we didn't part on the best of terms three years ago. I can understand that having the truth of your actions brought to light would've been upsetting for you, but this bizarre story you're concocting is beyond my understanding. I don't know what you mean to achieve by pursuing it—'

Astonishment lent strength to legs as she lurched upright. 'Wait a minute. Are you accusing me of making this up? Are you crazy?'

Rocco's head went up as if he'd been struck. 'On the contrary, I think you're the one who's impaired in some way.'

'Damn it, I am not making this up. You know I'm not!'

'Prove it. Show me some concrete evidence that my child is not in the care of a delusional excuse for a mother. Prove what you are saying or, so help me, I will take immediate steps to have him removed from your care.' He spoke in such a controlled, even tone and perversely that made Mia want to lash out at him even more.

Stark anger at his threat made her gasp in outrage. 'You bastard! You utterly heartless bastard. Haven't you done enough?'

'Obviously not. I should have kept a closer watch on you after we parted. You're not the first aggrieved 'ex-lover to attempt to keep a father from his child.' His jaw clenched hard on the words.

Mia clenched her fists and tried to take a deep breath. With every bone in her body, she wanted to tell him for the hundredth time to go to hell.

But what good would that achieve? Rocco had already been here far too long. Gianni had been asleep far longer than normal, but he wouldn't be asleep for much longer. And whatever the cost, she had to make sure Rocco wasn't here when her son woke up.

'You want evidence? I'll show it to you. But first I want something from you.'

'I don't think—'

'I don't care what you think. You claim you don't know what I'm talking about. Fine. I'll prove what I'm saying. But first, I want your written assurance that your being here won't be held against me in any way.'

She saw his puzzled frown and pre-empted his objection. 'Please spare me another I-have-no-idea-what-you're-talking-about episode. If you want to see the evidence, then you'll agree.'

After a terse silence, he nodded. 'Very well.'

She stifled a sigh of relief. 'Secondly, once I show it to you, I want you to leave.'

Immediately he shook his head. 'That would be impossible.'

'Then you leave me no choice.'

Trying to hide her trembling, she crossed the room and picked up the phone.

'What do you think you're doing?'

'I have an intruder in my house. I'm phoning the police.'

He didn't so much as flinch at her threat. 'Don't be stupid. How do you think the police will react when they find out just how long the intruder has been here?'

'Then go! I don't want you here.' Tears threatened, joining all the tumultuous emotions raging through her. 'Please, just go.'

For a beat he stared at her. Examined her face with an intensity that shook her insides. Then, he jerked out a nod. '*Va bene.* You have my word. I will leave once you show me this evidence you have. But before you look so pleased, rest assured, I will be back tomorrow morning, when I expect to be properly introduced to my son. After that we will have a long talk.'

'There's nothing to talk about.' Her voice held a desperate edge she prayed he hadn't picked up on.

'Show me the evidence, Mia.'

'Then you'll go?'

He heaved a frustrated breath. '*Sì.*'

She walked over to the cabinet set against one side of the tiny room. Opening the first drawer, she took out a key, which she used to open the second drawer. She hated the way her hands trembled as she pulled out the file, hated the way pain ripped through her as she nudged closed the drawer and turned around. Most of all, she hated the way Rocco stared so intently, witnessing every emotion she struggled not to feel as he held out his hand calmly for the file.

Taking it without a word, he retreated and seated himself on her favourite chair—and earned himself another black mark.

She stood in front of the cabinet and watched him leaf slowly through the file. He thumbed through copies of the emails she'd sent in desperation after he'd refused to take her calls; through photos his investigators had taken of her outside his office, chasing down his car on the road that last morning when he'd taken his private elevator to the garage instead of the front lobby as she'd been led to believe. That day she'd spent six hours in his reception waiting for a chance to speak to him, only to glance up and see him outside, preparing to slide into his Ferrari.

That memory brought a fresh wave of humiliation.

'Haven't you seen enough?' She moved to take the file from him.

He looked up. 'These pictures, when were they taken?'

'When do you think?' He continued to stare at her. 'Oh, for goodness' sake. There's a date stamp on the back.'

He flipped a few over and stared at the dates. 'This is dated six weeks after we parted.'

So he remembered when he'd ended their engagement? Why wouldn't he? He'd documented her every move to use as evidence against her. 'We didn't part, Rocco. You threw me out of the Palermo villa and the Milan apartment.'

The brief flare of his patrician nostrils was the only indication that he'd heard her. 'You remained in Milan all that time?' He was frowning again.

'I remained in Milan for two months, as you well know.'

He didn't answer this time as he set down one photo and picked up another. After examining each one, he finally picked up the transcript. Again he took his time reading the two-double-sided court document that forbade her from ever contacting Rocco Vitelli or coming within speaking distance of him.

Finally, he closed the file and stood. His face had grown gaunt; his pallor even more ashen, as if he'd received the worst shock of his life. But with his back against the window, Mia couldn't be certain. What she could see was that he was staring at the file as if it were an alien being.

'Makes grim reading, doesn't it, seeing it all in black and white? Now that you've refreshed your memory, can you please go?'

He lifted his gaze to her and Mia bit back a gasp at the stark torment in the dark depths of his eyes. When he exhaled, it emerged a harsh, cracked sound.

'I have no idea who did this to you, Mia. But it wasn't me.'

CHAPTER FOUR

'EXCUSE ME?' MIA was sure her hearing was playing tricks on her.

'This—' Rocco lifted the file '—was not my doing.' His voice was as stark as the look in his eyes. With abrupt movements he slammed the file on the chair. 'I swear it.'

Light-headed with the rapid drain of blood from her head, she swayed against the cabinet. 'This is not your doing,' she echoed the words through numb lips. Her brain struggled even harder to grasp their meaning.

'No. It is not.' He advanced as he spoke until he stood right in front of her. Up close, she could see the terrible tension that gripped his face, held his body taut. 'If the evidence in that file is to be believed…' he paused at her outraged gasp '…then someone has perpetrated a terrible injustice on both of us.'

'Someone?' She'd found her voice, even though it emerged higher than she would have wished. 'You seriously expect me to believe that this had nothing to do with you? That someone *else* did this? How stupid do you think I am?'

He let out another harsh breath and grasped her arms.

'You need to calm down so we can talk about this rationally.'

'No!' She wrenched herself away from him. 'Enough. Please, enough. Whatever game you're playing, it's gone on long enough. You said you'd leave once I showed you the evidence. You've seen it. Now leave.' She was hanging by a thread, and she didn't know how much more she could take. Rushing to the door on unsteady feet, she reached for the doorknob.

'I understand you're emotional—'

She rounded on him. 'Of course I'm emotional. I'm human, not a robot like you. I don't revel in mind games the way you do. At least have the decency not to insult my intelligence. You know every single shred of evidence in that file is the truth. The charges may have been trumped up, but it's based on the truth, or a twisted version of it. I sent you those emails. I made those phone calls. I camped outside your office for a chance to talk to you. For two months I tried to get you to talk to me, and I used every means available to me because I thought you had the right to know about your unborn child. But to use it against me that way? To accuse me of stalking?' She stopped to swallow a sob that threatened to escape. 'You disgust me, you know that?'

'*Basta!* If you would just calm down and think this through properly, you'll realise I speak the truth.'

'No. You listen to me for a change. I want you out of my house, and out of my life. Here, take the file with you. You can refresh your memory over a glass of Chianti. But know this. If you ever turn up on my doorstep again, I will take action against you for harassment.'

Her rant went unanswered as he slowly dug his hand

into his breast pocket. 'Did you hear what I said?' she demanded, fighting a wave of hysteria that threatened to suck her under.

When his hand emerged, he held his passport. He turned to retrieve the file. 'Come here.' His terse command achieved the opposite. She held her ground and remained by the door. After a moment, he looked up. 'Mia, if you want this nightmare to end for both of us, indulge me for a moment. *Per favore.*'

Against her better judgement, she moved towards him, morbid curiosity biting into her. He had the file opened to where his statement was etched in grim black and white. Words like *dangerous*, *unhinged*, *obsessed* jumped out at her and she cringed as tears prickled behind her eyes.

Rocco flipped the statement to the last page. Opening his passport, he held it next to his signed statement. 'Do you see a difference?'

Blinking, she frowned. 'What am I supposed to be looking at?'

'Purportedly, I signed this statement, no? Look at the signature in my passport. Now look at the two signatures and tell me what you see.'

She looked closer. A tingle shot down her spine and a strange buzz started in her head as the pages blurred. Blinking hard, she stared, her eyes darting between the two documents. Slowly, the implications began to sink in.

She raised her gaze to him. 'Are…are you saying this is not your signature?'

He gave a grim nod. *'Io sono spiacente.'*

It took another few seconds for his meaning to sink

in. She flew at him, landing blows everywhere she could reach. 'You're sorry?' she shrieked. 'For over three years I've lived in fear of being hauled off to jail on a whim, lived in fear of losing my child in case I somehow violate the terms of the restraining order... and all you can say is, you're sorry?' Tears streamed down her face as her emotions finally burst their bank.

Rocco didn't move. Not a muscle as her anger and despair ripped free. Finally, overcome by racking sobs, she collapsed against him. Then he caught her to him, holding her in his arms as she shuddered with emotional overload. Through her distress, she heard him murmur soft words in Italian, words meant to soothe, but that only made her cry harder as she continued to slam her fists against his arms, shoulders, anywhere she could reach, until she was drained and wretched.

It was only when her tears lessened to unladylike hiccups, that she heard it. The sound she should have been listening out for. The sound that should have been her first concern in all this madness.

The impatient wail that was Gianni's waking call.

She wrenched herself out of Rocco's arms and stumbled backwards. 'Go. Now!'

'*Cara*, you are not in a state to be left—'

'No, you said you would leave. You promised!'

'*Sì*, and I will, when you've calmed down.'

Gianni let out another plaintive cry. Torn between going to her son and making sure his father disappeared as quickly as he'd arrived, she paused. And nearly jumped out of her skin when the doorbell pealed. With a sharp cry, she whirled towards it. The hand that closed over her shoulder stopped her in her tracks.

'Go and get the boy. I will get the door.' Rocco's authoritative voice was couched in helpful charm. As much as she wanted to tell him to go to hell, Gianni's demand to be let out of his cot was getting to the stage where Mia knew that if she didn't get upstairs immediately, he'd attempt to climb out himself.

Reluctantly, she nodded, and, swallowing down the last of her hiccups, she headed for the stairs.

'Mia?'

She turned to find him behind her, pulling out a cotton square from his pocket, which he held out to her. 'Unless you want to upset our son, I suggest you try and remove some of the evidence of your distress.'

Belatedly, she lifted a hand to her face and realised her cheeks were still wet with her tears, not to mention her runny nose that must make her resemble a wet scarecrow. With a deep flush engulfing her face, she snatched the handkerchief, not bothering to murmur her thanks as she fled up the stairs.

She'd reached the top of the stairs when she heard Mrs Hart greeting Rocco as if they were old friends.

Pursing her lips at the further unwanted intrusion, she hurried down the hall and arrived in time to see Gianni swing one plump leg over the top of the cot, ready to escape his perceived prison.

She rushed to him and swung him into her arms. 'No, no, sweetheart. I told you, you mustn't do that.'

Hiding her face against his chubby neck, she hugged him close to her, all her anger and anxiety draining out of her to be replaced by the rush of love she felt for her little boy.

When he pulled at her hair and repeated her words—

'No, no, tweehar…'—her smile wobbled and she clutched him closer. He protested and began to squirm.

But knowing what faced her downstairs, Mia held on for a moment longer, selfishly basking in her son's innocence until he wriggled harder, eager to be set free.

'All right. But you know the drill. First a nappy change. Okay?'

Immediately he shook his head. 'No nappy.'

Her smile widened. 'Yes nappy, then you can play with your racing cars.'

It could've been the change in his normal routine or the instinctive warning that all was not right with his mother. But far from crowing with joy the way he normally did at the prospect of playing with his beloved racing cars instead of sitting in his high chair in the kitchen for his pre-dinner fruit plate, he regarded his mother solemnly for several seconds with a gaze so shrewd and reminiscent of his father's, Mia's heart twisted in pain.

Then a smile broke over his face. 'Racing car!'

'Yes, but first, nappy change.'

And then, please, God, let Rocco have disappeared quietly without making a fuss by the time she returned downstairs. The notion that she was grasping at straws stayed with her as she changed Gianni's nappy, but she refused to let go of the hope as she clutched her son— who in turn clutched one yellow and one red racing car in his fists—and made her way downstairs.

With each step she recalled her conversation with Rocco just before Gianni woke up. Was it true? Had someone instigated the accusations against her, dragged her to court under fabricated charges, all without Rocco knowing? That seemed too unthinkable, so impossible, that she couldn't begin to wrap her head around it. She paused as another, equally unthinkable, thought struck her.

If Rocco hadn't known of his son's existence, what would he do now that he knew? The image of his face when she accused him of knowing and deliberately ignoring Gianni's existence rose in her mind.

What had he said?

You think anything will come between me and my flesh and blood?

What did that mean? Her veins filled with ice as possible new interpretations tumbled through her mind. Did Rocco mean to take her son away from her? Somehow declare her an unfit mother and demand full custody and spirit her son away to Italy?

Suddenly desperate to know his intentions, she hitched Gianni securely onto her hip and clambered down the remaining stairs.

Only to find her prayers had been answered.

Her living room was empty.

After a rough night where tossing and turning had alternated with anxious pacing in the close confines of her bedroom, dawn came with Mia being no further enlightened as to Rocco's true intentions. Was he coming back? Or was he going to disappear just as quickly as he'd appeared, leaving her life in even deeper turmoil?

Somewhere in the long dark, daunting hours of the night, she'd realised that she'd been too distressed to question him further when he'd claimed he'd had nothing to do with the restraining order under whose shadow she'd lived for over three years. As the weak sunlight snuck around her curtains, she also realised she was still as in the dark about every charge thrown at her as she'd been when she'd demanded Rocco leave.

If *he* hadn't instigated those charges against her, who had? And to what end? It turned her blood cold at the thought of someone being so cruel, as to do that to her and her unborn child.

During her time in Italy, first as Rocco's structural engineer on his latest resort-building project, and later as his fiancée, she'd met countless people who inevitably passed through the life of an influential and powerful billionaire. Most had been pleasant, some not so much, but wracking her brain, as she'd done many times during the night, she'd come away with nothing but a throbbing headache.

Rocco's cousin Alessandro, and his wife, Allegra, had been cool and dismissive towards her when Rocco had moved her from his Milan apartment into the Palermo villa he shared with his *nonna* soon after their engagement. With Alessandro's departure for Brazil where, as Rocco's right-hand man, he'd been spearheading the push of Vitelli Construction into Latin America, their relationship had never truly blossomed. If Mia was honest, she'd never felt any genuine warmth from Alessandro, but she wouldn't have stooped so far as to accuse him of orchestrating such a hideous vendetta against her.

Which brought her to another dilemma. If the order and charges against her were bogus, trying to overturn them would involve hiring a lawyer or a private investigator to prove her innocence and that, of course, would cost money. Precious money she couldn't afford.

So she was back to square one. She had no means of fighting the injustice done against her, no way of proving it unless she found the money from somewhere.

She was still burning millions of brain cells over the issue when her doorbell rang just after nine. Setting Gianni's breakfast of Marmite soldiers down in front of him, she brushed crumbs from her fingers and went to answer it.

Rocco stood on her doorstep, large, imposing and dangerously handsome, dressed from head to toe in black. Her stomach executed a perfect triple somersault, the blood rushing through her veins at the speed of light, both independent actions causing her a light-headedness that had her clinging to the doorknob for support.

He really had no right to look this good first thing in the morning, she thought bitterly, especially when she knew she looked far less than her best, her brief glimpse of herself in the bathroom mirror as she'd splashed water on her face having confirmed that fact.

'You look like you're going to a funeral. And did your hearing die along with your conscience? I distinctly recall asking you not to come back.' The words spilt from her lips before she could stop them but she refused to take them back, simply because she hated the way he made her heart beat twice as fast just with his presence; hated the way he made every cell in her body sing with life and her legs turn to jelly just by being there; she hated the way he seemed to glow with life when she felt worse than death. Most of all she hated the clamouring instinct that warned her he wasn't here to enquire about her health.

'Still get testy when you don't get enough sleep?' he countered smoothly, his lips twitching with amusement, before slipping his impressive bulk past her to enter her cottage.

'Whether I did or not is nothing to do with you,' she forced through clenched teeth only to grit them further when he sent her a mocking glance. 'What are you doing here anyway?' Conscious of Gianni in the next room, she tried for an even tone, even though she wanted to shriek the words at him.

'You really expect me to stay away after what I discovered yesterday?' he questioned, incredulous.

She turned to shut the door, taking a few precious moments to regroup. When she turned, he was facing her, his intense blue eyes narrowed as he raked her from head to toe. The scrutiny did nothing to ease the pounding in her chest or the sudden careening of butterflies in her stomach when his return gaze paused for an indecent amount of time on her breasts.

'I was hoping you'd respect my wishes, yes.' Her voice emerged shaky and slightly feeble. She cursed herself. And him. His ability to upset her equilibrium with just a look wasn't going down well in light of her tumultuous feelings this morning.

'Don't be so naïve, Mia. I have a son whose existence I've only just been made aware of. I intend to form a relationship with him. Unfortunately for you, no amount of wishing on your part will make that fact disappear. I've already informed Nonna that her suspicions were right.'

Where she'd failed miserably, his tone was smooth and even, moderated, she suspected, for the sake of Gianni, who was banging on his high chair in the kitchen.

As if pulled by a magnet, Rocco turned towards the sound.

'Wait,' she whispered urgently, although she knew she was only delaying the inevitable.

'No. I will not wait,' he sliced at her, his voice gruff with emotion.

She bit back a shocked gasp at the dark torment in his eyes when he speared her gaze with his.

'I've been kept in the dark for three years. Whoever is at fault will pay for that, never doubt it, but I will not wait one second longer to meet my son.'

His long legs carried him to the kitchen in six easy strides. By the time Mia joined him, he was already kneeling in front of Gianni.

Once again father and son regarded each other with equal fascination. And once again, Mia's heart hammered until she was sure it would burst out of her chest.

'*Buongiorno*, Gianni. *Io sono papà*. I am your father.' The raw words, spoken with a tortured mixture of pride and pain, tore through Mia.

As if he understood the profound words, Gianni nodded. His lower lip pouted, then trembled. Rocco lifted a slightly trembling hand and touched his son's cheek. Gianni's pout deepened. Mia held her breath, ready to scoop up her child at the slightest sign of distress but, thankfully, no tears arrived. She stayed by the door, her heart in her throat.

Gently, Rocco moved his hand up and stroked Gianni's curls, all the while drinking in his features as if to imprint them on his brain. He whispered soft, incoherent words to his son, which must have soothed him, because gradually Gianni's pout retracted, to be replaced by curiosity. When Rocco's hand returned to his cheek, Gianni reciprocated the gesture by picking up a piece of toast and shoving it in his father's face.

Warm, hoarse laughter broke from Rocco's throat as he caught the food between his teeth and munched with relish. Breaking into a grin, Gianni picked up another piece and repeated the gesture.

Turning away from the heart-wrenching scene for fear that her son would witness her tears, she busied herself fetching his small pot of yoghurt from the fridge.

Behind her father and son deepened their instant bonding by murmuring adorable rubbish to each other. With every soft word uttered, every murmur of appreciation for what a clever child he was—it was amazing how quickly her understanding of Italian rushed back when it counted—her heart crumbled further.

A wave of shame washed over her as she admitted that some small part of her had hoped her Gianni would hate his father on sight. But really, would that have made things easier? Rocco was nothing if not a ruthless fighter. After all, weren't his sharp mind and extreme risk-taking in architecture what had made her seek out a job in his company fresh out of university? If he hadn't bonded instantly with his son, he wouldn't have given up. And a determined Rocco was a formidable force to be reckoned with. So perhaps it was easier this way.

She turned from the fridge to find him wiping the

excess Marmite from his son's chin. Sensing her gaze, he glanced up.

Instantly his soft look disappeared. 'We need to talk.' He stood to tower over her, his even tone belying the piercing intent in his eyes.

There was no escaping the inevitable. 'I need to feed him his yoghurt.'

Her stalling tactic failed as he reached out a hand and smoothly relieved her of the small tub. 'I'll take care of it. You can use the time to pack a bag—'

She snatched in a shocked breath. 'Pack a bag? If you think I'm going anywhere with you, you need your head examined.' Realising her son was studying her with intense fascination, she struggled to smile through clenched teeth. 'We can talk here.'

When he reached out again, she tensed, afraid of what direct contact with his touch might do to her crumbling state of mind. But he merely reached past her to grab a plastic spoon off the counter. His eyes mocked her as he read her reaction.

'Easy, *cara*. You've developed a penchant for over-reacting at the slightest opportunity—'

'Can you blame me? I've lived in fear of being imprisoned for the last three years!'

A spasm of some unknown emotion raced across his face but was gone too quickly for her to decipher, although the intensity in his face eased. 'I merely wanted you to pack a bag for Gianni since we'll be gone most of the day.'

She crossed her arms defensively. 'And where exactly are we going?'

'I delivered your file to my lawyers last night. They

assure me that this is the first time they're aware of this document, which confirms my suspicion that the case against you is a fraudulent one.'

The mingled shock and relief that spiked through her lasted for a mere second but nevertheless it caused her to lose what little feeling she had in her legs. She started to sag against the sink.

Rocco's hands arrived at her waist, easily holding her up. 'Are you all right?'

She shook her head, wisely extricated herself from his hold, and cleared her throat before attempting to speak. Still her voice emerged as hollow as a discarded seashell. 'Are you saying that all this time, all the threats, the letters, my living in fear…were all for nothing?'

A grim look crossed Rocco's face as he returned to his task of spooning yoghurt into his son's waiting mouth. 'I have no doubt that whoever sent them meant for you to take them seriously.'

'But who would do that?' Sheer disbelief gave way to anger so deep she shook with it. Taking a deep breath, she struggled to hold herself together.

Rocco continued to feed Gianni, although his massive shoulders lifted in a shrug underneath the stretch of expensive black suit. 'I have a lot of enemies. Unfortunately, it goes with the territory where money and power are involved. Someone must have believed they could get to me through you. Or vice versa.'

His words made tears prickle and her laugh grated painfully in her own ears. 'But they couldn't have been more wrong, could they? You wanted nothing to do with me after your precious blueprints went missing and you were forced to halt construction of the Abu Dhabi project. In fact, I'm surprised you didn't think of this sort of punishment yourself.'

He stiffened as if a bolt of electricity had shot through him, but his face gave nothing away. With casual ease, he continued to feed his son until the pot was empty. Then he put it to one side and cleaned up the remnants of Gianni's breakfast as efficiently as if he'd been doing it since he was born.

As she watched him, the small part of Mia not reeling with shock and hurt found it hard to believe Rocco had only just met his son. And the realisation of how keenly and naturally Rocco had taken to fatherhood sent a spike of alarm through her, effectively blotting out the niggling that had started at the back of her mind.

Rocco picked up a red racing car off the counter and handed it to his son, brushing his hand affectionately through his hair before turning to her.

'The women I associate with are normally well aware of the terms of our association. Yours was the only alliance I had a little…difficulty with.'

Heat rushed up her face at the deliberate barb, but she forced her chin up. 'I'm sorry if I didn't just slink away quietly when accused of being a thief! I wouldn't have been able to live with myself if I hadn't tried to defend myself.'

'That's a very admirable quality, in the right circumstances. Unfortunately, when the weight of evidence is against you, sometimes it's better to make a quiet exit than to draw even more attention to yourself.'

'And be labelled a thief for the rest of my life? No one would've hired me. You certainly weren't inclined to give me a reference and you made sure I was black-listed everywhere. So, tell me, where would that have left me?'

Narrowed eyes threatened to tear strips off her skin. 'Married to a billionaire, if you'd only kept your mouth shut and not further compromised your situation by revealing your true intentions before my wedding ring was on your finger. That way you'd have been set for life, wouldn't you?' His words were by no less deadly for their soft delivery.

Confusion caused her to frown. 'What are you talking about?' she demanded.

He ignored her question and glanced at his watch. 'We have an appointment with my lawyers at one o'clock. If we are to make it, I suggest you get a move on.'

The mercurial direction of the conversation was causing her head to spin. 'Your lawyers? Why would they want to meet with me?'

'This is now officially a fraud investigation. You need to provide a formal statement.' His eyes flicked to Gianni and the ruthless determination in their depths caused her heart to miss several beats.

'Why wasn't I consulted before you arranged any of this? You can't just blow into my life after making it a living hell and start making decisions without my consent. Besides, everything you need is in that file. That should be enough.' Her voice had been rising with her agitation and, belatedly, she noted Gianni staring at her, his lower lip beginning to tremble. She rushed forward and scooped him out of his chair. Murmuring soft words to him, she glared at Rocco over his head.

He leaned back against the small counter and crossed his legs at the ankles, but his easy stance didn't fool her for a second. 'Perhaps I was wrong, but I was under the impression that the chance to clear your name would please you, not cause you so much distress.'

'I'm not distressed! I'm angry,' she hissed at him. 'You can't just swoop in out of nowhere after three years and start laying down the law like some…like some…' The word she wanted to utter wouldn't have been suitable for her son's innocent ears, so she contented herself with an even more withering glare.

Rocco merely folded lean, muscled arms over his chest and regarded her steadily. 'So I take it you don't want to clear your name? That you'd rather live with this "obsessive stalker" label hanging over your head?'

She yearned to claw the mockery out of his eyes, pound her fists against his chest for taunting her into falling in with his plans. But with her son in her arms, she had to content herself with an even fiercer glare before, walking out of the kitchen, she placed Gianni on his play mat in front of the unlit fireplace.

Turning, she found Rocco directly behind her. Every essence of his masculine aura filling every angle of her vision so completely, she had to force herself to concentrate on what she'd been about to say.

'I hate you,' she husked out with as much feeling as she could muster without distressing her son.

His eyes glinted with dark amusement. 'I take it that's a yes, then?'

Her hands balled into fists. 'Of course I want to get to clear my name. That doesn't mean I'm willing to let you ride roughshod over me to do it.'

In a flash, his expression altered. His mouth softened into a sensual curve and his eyes blazed a long-forgotten hunger that made the muscles of her stomach dance crazily.

'I seem to recall there were two things that could hold your utter attention: sex and work. While I enjoyed our mental grappling in the boardroom, I found the bedroom games just as stimulating.' His hands slid over her waist to cup her bottom, bringing her into sharp contact with his groin and the masculine dominance of his erection. His mouth descended, a sensual promise that came to hover deliciously over her lips. 'In the bedroom we had perfect understanding, *cara*, and if that's the only way I can get your cooperation, and stop you spitting nails at me, then I'm willing to try it.'

'Don't go martyring yourself for my sake.' The sarcasm she aimed at him emerged high-pitched and desperately false.

He laughed low in his throat, the sound singing along her nerves in ways that did nothing to soothe her equilibrium.

'Trust me, it won't be a hardship at all. I told you last night, the body doesn't lie and right now mine is demanding that I be true to it in the most primal way.' One hand caressed its way up her side, sparking flash fires wherever he touched. When it curved beneath the soft swell of her breast, she knew she had to do something or risk dissolving into a heated puddle at his feet.

The hands she lifted to push him away with felt feeble. 'Aren't you forgetting something?'

He lifted winged brows, even as his mouth descended another tempting millimetre, his warm breath washing over her tingling lips, setting them on fire so she had to fight not to give into the temptation to lick moisture into them.

'You threw me out of your life three years ago. You warned me never to darken your door again, remember?' Her voice emerged husky, heavy with a need she was fighting desperately to deny.

'Not because I had grown tired of the exquisite pleasure I found in your body. In fact, that was the reason I swore never to set foot in England again.'

She was shocked by this stark admission; her eyes flew to his. 'You couldn't trust yourself to be around me, despite labelling me as a thief?'

A grim smile twitched his lips. 'You see what the power of sex can do? Even in the midst of bitter disillusionment and betrayal, the body wants what it wants.' To demonstrate, he brought her closer still to his tight, masculine form so she could not fail to feel the evidence for herself.

'God, you make it sound so cheap and sordid!'

'Deny it if you must, but it's the truth.' This time his lips lowered enough to brush over hers.

The brief contact sent a wild shudder through her, the force of her own need stabbing her deep in the pelvis. A moan of pleasure escaped before she could stop it. When he lifted his head, she realised her hands had curled into his chest. She straightened them, but found she couldn't quite remove them from the heated, cotton-covered flesh.

'Don't do this, Rocco. If this is the example you're hoping to set your son, then I pray for his upbringing.'

If she'd meant the words to cause offence, she was

disappointed. In true Latin style, he shrugged eloquently.

'It's right for him to learn that feelings should be expressed naturally. I don't want him to be brought up with the suppressing of feelings and stiff-upper-lip nonsense you English are so fond of. It's also good for him to see that his parents can express natural feelings towards one another.'

She knew he meant this as she'd witnessed, and envied, the open love and warmth he shared with his grandmother and cousins. But still, 'I wouldn't describe what I'm feeling for you right now as natural.'

Raising his head, he feathered a forefinger down her cheek, his lips curving with a hint of a smile she recalled as devastating when fully unfurled. 'Really? How would you describe it?'

'Murderous is a good start,' she forced out, despite the battle she fought against the urge to curl into his touch.

He tossed out another shrug, in no way disturbed by her answer. 'You're not the first to want my head on a platter.'

'You mean I'm not the first person to be falsely accused of stealing by you?'

Where the first reminder had failed miserably, this second reminder of why he'd thrown her out of his life succeeded. Like a switch, the heat was extinguished from his eyes. Mia should've been thankful that she'd achieved her aim, but all she felt was bereft when his arms fell from her. She cursed herself for her weakness. Why? After all he'd done to her, couldn't she summon enough willpower to resist him?

'Perhaps you're right. Some things should not be aired in front of my son.'

My son.

The fierce possession in his statement fired a warning in Mia's head. *He's my son too*, she wanted to rage at him, but Gianni had already been bombarded with too many emotions this morning and her normally chatty son was now gazing solemnly at his parents. It irked her that Rocco was right, that she hadn't considered her son's feelings before she'd let herself be dragged into a heated exchange in his presence.

But then he'd always had that effect on her, hadn't he? His lean, dark, heart-stopping good looks combined with that hard muscle-packed body had spelt trouble for her the first time she'd laid eyes on him two months into her employment with the London division of Vitelli Construction. But it was the deadly combination of that and his superior intellect that had tipped her over the edge of uncontrollable lust into full-blown infatuation.

And hadn't he fed into it? He'd lapped it up as if it were his due, taken everything she had to offer and more, until she'd felt herself disappearing into the giant, larger than life force that was Rocco Vitelli.

It enraged her now to think she'd come so close to giving up everything, every damn thing she'd worked so hard for, to please him. Only to find out the real reason for his proposal: first as a means of pleasing his grandmother, and then, provided nature took its course—and why shouldn't it, since Rocco Vitelli willed it?—as a breeding machine to carry on the Vitelli empire.

Of course, in the end it hadn't mattered because clever, quick-thinking and infinitely superior Rocco had got the boot in first and she'd been forced to give up everything anyway. The career she'd so carefully planned and proudly achieved *in spite* of her every misgiving, *in spite* of the very loud echoes about her unworthiness, had been ripped from her in the blink of an eye.

Except now he was dangling the carrot of getting her life back, to put the horror of the last three years behind her. Was she a fool to refuse this chance to finally move on with her life, to start providing for her son the way she'd been unable to do since he was born? She could wallow in bitterness for what had happened to her, or she could dust herself off, accept his offer of assistance and start reclaiming her life.

'How long will we be gone?' she asked, after taking a steadying breath.

The barest hint of tension eased from his frame. A minuscule signal that he wasn't blasé about all this. For some absurd reason, it eased Mia's knotted insides.

'If everything goes according to plan, the business side of things should be concluded in a few hours,' he replied.

By teatime she could be free of the nightmare that'd been hanging over her for three long years.

Of course, it wasn't till much later that the full meaning of his words truly sank in.

CHAPTER FIVE

ROCCO'S GAZE TRACKED Mia as she walked away from him.

Last night he'd barely slept. Finding out you had a son and discovering the nefarious circumstances that had kept his birth from you had a way of depriving a man of sleep in a way the strongest caffeine or most challenging boardroom negotiations could not achieve. Anger, shock and a sense of profound loss had all wrestled for equal chunks of him.

But in the end, steely resolution had won out.

He had a son. And he intended to claim him, by any means possible.

He walked over and crouched down in front of Gianni, his heart once again overwhelmed by the miracle in front of him. Plump hands lifted up the red racing car to him. He accepted it, swallowing the lump in his throat before settling himself on the floor in front of him.

He had a son who had surpassed all goals to become his number one priority. And for now he had to recognise that mother and son came as a package, which meant any plans he had for Gianni would have to include Mia. He'd known what he needed to do even before he'd picked up the phone to confirm the news to Nonna.

His grandmother's sobs of happiness had brought a brief smile to his own lips and alleviated any guilt he felt about what he had to do to secure his place in his son's life.

The Mia he knew had always been feisty, fighting her corner, whether in the boardroom or against his absolute possession of her in the bedroom, so he had a fight on his hands to convince Mia to fall in with his plans.

And in light of what she'd been through—an ordeal that would've cowed most people but evidently not Mia, since she'd remained impressively, admirably spirited—he had to tread carefully. But, ultimately, he was determined to win.

First, he would restore all that had been ripped away from her three years ago. As she'd proved with resounding success to him, money and privilege were a potent aphrodisiac, dispensing with even the staunchest of beliefs. All he had to do was set her dreams in front of her to have her.

Fate, if you believed in that sort of thing, had taken care of her one objection to their previous relationship. She'd been willing to enjoy the influence and power his position brought, but not the child she'd known he'd ultimately wanted.

What had pained him most then and continued to disillusion him now was that she'd been so engrossed in trying to clear her name, so intent on salvaging her career, she'd brushed aside his shocked demand.

His lips thinned in memory of their confrontation that last morning.

Of course, I didn't want to have your child!

The words still had the power to freeze his insides, the callous words raw and bruisingly bracing in ways he'd never imagined possible.

So why had she gone ahead with the pregnancy?

Had she had a change of heart the moment she'd known she was carrying his child? Or had she needed convincing? How had she coped with the pregnancy itself? With firm resolution, he pushed away the questions. He was burning to know the answers but the reality of his son made them less urgent. The promise he'd made to Nonna had been fulfilled, even without him realising it.

And now he'd been blessed with this gift, he intended to hang onto it with both hands.

Mia stood in front of her wardrobe, eyeing its meagre contents with increasing anxiety. Although why she should be anxious about meeting a bunch of lawyers, she had no idea. Surely she should be celebrating the fact that her name was about to be cleared? She could finally move on with her life and take proper care of her son without having to worry. So why was she stressing over what to wear?

Biting her lip, she acknowledged her anxiety stemmed from another source. Rocco hadn't mentioned his plans concerning Gianni. And after witnessing the depths of Rocco's emotions both yesterday and this morning, and the instant bond between father and son, she'd be naïve to think Rocco wouldn't demand some sort of contact with Gianni.

The thought of being parted from her son for even a minute tore her insides to shreds.

Maybe she was jumping the gun, she mused impatiently as she whipped the only decent outfit—a knee-length navy-blue dress with a crossover bodice that had seen better days—off the hanger. The soft jersey material would have to do the job of keeping her warm, especially since she'd been putting off buying tights until the weather got really cold. She located her black-heeled pumps at the back of the wardrobe, slipped them on and took a few experimental steps to the window and back. Having lived in flats and trainers since Gianni's birth, the last thing she wanted to do was to topple over in her three-inch heels with her son in her arms.

Confident she could carry it off without coming across like a limping ostrich, she brushed her hair, smoothed on a trace of gloss and re-hung the clothes she'd strewn on the bed. Checking her appearance one last time, she slipped into Gianni's room and picked up the bag she'd packed for him.

The sound of laughter reached her ears as she descended the stairs.

The first thing she saw was Rocco's legs splayed out, followed by powerful thighs, lean tapered hips and impressive torso, on which lay her son, giggling uncontrollably at the faces his father, sprawled out on her living room floor, was pulling.

It took several moments for them to realise they had an audience, and several more for the humour to be wiped from Rocco's eyes. In those moments, she was reminded of when they'd been together, sharing a joke, or laughing for no reason, simply because she was happy.

The painful reminder delivered a punch so forceful to her midsection, she struggled to catch her breath.

'I… I'm ready,' she said, her voice scratchy with torn emotions.

She wanted to hate Rocco, she really did. But now she was presented with the picture of an indulgent father and content son, her heart flipped in a way that sent huge alarm bells through her brain.

Her heart took a further hammering when he sat up easily, one strong arm secure around his son as he rose fluidly to his feet and raked a tidying hand through his hair, looking sexily and sinfully dishevelled as he stared down at her.

'Ah. Your mamma has decided to grace us with her presence.' Dark blue eyes gleamed as they raked her form, lingering over her cleavage and hips in ways that made her hot all over.

Gianni beamed his approval. 'Mummy…lovely,' he said.

Setting down the bag before it fell from her suddenly clammy fingers, she reached for Gianni. 'I changed him just before breakfast so he doesn't need changing. I'll just put his sweater on and we can be on our way.'

Rocco handed him over, but his gaze stayed on hers for a charged second, sending spikes of heat through her and bringing thoughts of their earlier conversation flooding through her. She felt his gaze on her as she carried Gianni over to the sofa, sat him down and pulled his sweater over the long sleeve T-shirt and jeans he wore.

When she looked up, Rocco had the door open and the case in his hand. 'I'll take him so you can lock up.'

Unused to having another adult presence in Gianni's life since her grandmother's death, and feeling bereft at being relieved of him so quickly, she hesitated.

Rocco's eyes narrowed and the last of the warmth left his face. 'I'm not going to spirit him away the second your back is turned, if that's what you think.'

But that was just the problem. She had no idea what to think, since she had no idea what role he intended to play in his son's life. Biting her lips over her jumbled emotions, she handed Gianni to him, fished her keys out of her bag and locked the door behind her.

She approached the car in time to see him settle Gianni into a brand-new car seat. Seeing her surprise, he raised his brows in query.

'Did you think I would forget such an important safety issue?' he drawled.

If she was honest, yes, although now she thought of it, she realised Rocco, with his menagerie of nieces and nephews produced by his extended family, had more experience with children than she'd ever had, and the thought caused her even more worry.

Sliding into the silver Bentley to sit opposite her son, she felt unmoored, as if her life were spiralling out of her control, which was ridiculous. All he'd done was buy her son a car seat. Nothing wildly strange about that, she assured herself.

'I flew in by helicopter this morning, but as I wasn't sure how Gianni would react to the flight, I suggest we travel by road.'

Gianni would've probably loved it, but since *she*

hadn't been keen on Rocco's helicopter rides during the times she'd had to accompany him on site visits, she nodded. 'It's probably best.'

She crossed her legs and immediately uncrossed them when her calf brushed the warm material of his trousers. Heat, delicious and stinging, raced along her skin, tightening her nipples into painful points. The immediacy of the reaction sent a gasp flying from her lips. And the thought that she had to endure almost two hours of Rocco's dark, masculine presence sent a moan chasing after it.

'I would ask you what is wrong, *cara*, but I already know. I felt it too.' Molten eyes the colour of a storm-tossed sea speared her with flames of desire.

She swallowed hard. 'Whatever I feel...whatever you feel, this is going nowhere,' she warned, more to herself, she suspected, than to him.

His eyes dropped to her mouth, lingered for tense, dangerous seconds, before arriving back to hers. 'We shall see.'

The words sounded so very much like a challenge, Mia swallowed again. Her gaze fell on her son and she breathed a sigh of relief. While Gianni was in the car with them, Rocco would not try anything.

Would he?

She cast him a furtive glance and caught his gaze on her face. Reading her features clearly, he smiled. It was a wholly untamed, deeply devastating smile that reeked of masculine arrogance.

Colour shot up her face, but she raised her chin and stared him down. After several seconds he turned his gaze on Gianni.

For several miles he entertained Gianni, leaving Mia to suffer his more than occasional, seemingly innocent contact every time he adjusted his large frame. And with each brush of body against hers, she experienced a bone-deep tingle that reignited primal sensations and a fierce yearning to pull closer to the powerful, masculine temptation that was Rocco.

Instead, she forced her hands to stayed curled in her lap, her attention on the grey motorway that whizzed past her window.

'*Grazie.*' The pull of his scrutiny, accompanied by the solemnly uttered word, drew her attention. She turned to see his gaze shift from his dozing son's smooth, innocent face to hers. As much as she tried not to be affected by the hypnotic gleam in their stormy depths, several missed heartbeats told her she hadn't been successful.

'For what?' she asked with genuine puzzlement.

'For naming Gianni after my grandfather. He's an exceptional boy. Nonna will be so proud.' There was a discernible vein of pride in his voice coupled with a fierce possessiveness.

She couldn't help the blush that suffused her face, and nor could she pull her gaze from his compelling eyes that made deadly promises she knew he wouldn't deliver, no matter how difficult. God, hadn't she learned her lesson?

Pushing down her despair, she answered with a thin shrug. 'I know how much your grandmother misses your grandfather, even after all these years. I… I hoped this might in some way help her cope with her loss.'

Rocco's grandfather had died very young from a sudden heart attack, when Rocco was only nine. His grandmother had never remarried and had chosen instead to bring up her orphaned grandchild by herself, working her fingers to the bone to provide for him.

Rocco's eyes narrowed on her, a small amount of surprise and a healthy dose of suspicion in his gaze. 'And how do you know this?'

'Caterina told me how your grandfather died, and how she knew from the first time she met him that he was the only man for her.' Mia also remembered how her heart had sung at the time because she'd believed she had same in Giovanni Vitelli's grandson.

How wrong she'd been!

Puzzlement replaced the suspicion in Rocco's eyes, prompting her to ask, 'What?'

'I did not know you had such intimate conversations with my grandmother.' His frown evidenced his obvious displeasure at the knowledge and Mia couldn't defend herself against the barb of hurt that pierced her.

To hide it, she lifted her chin. 'There were a lot of things you didn't bother to find out about me, Rocco, starting with the misconception that I was a thief.'

His jaw immediately tightened, an accurate sign that her barb had hit home. 'The evidence against you was real. I had proof. My competitors came into possession of the blueprints the same day you attended the meeting. A source confirmed you were in possession of it when you arrived.'

'That's a lie!' For the millionth time, Mia wracked her brain for why someone had concocted such a web of lies against her, but she came up empty. She shook her head to clear the memories and to think straight beneath the intensity of Rocco's condemning scrutiny. 'The only thing I had in my possession when I arrived for that meeting was my briefcase containing my laptop and portfolio. And as far as I know, toying with looking and being offered a job isn't a crime.'

'But you didn't tell me you were looking for a job. You hid it from me until I confronted you with it.'

Mia inhaled slowly as remembered regret flooded her. Looking for another job had been the last thing she'd wanted, but with the Vitelli Construction office grapevine blazing with speculation as to how she'd landed the job working with Rocco, she'd known to preserve her professional integrity she either had to find another position or end her relationship with Rocco. The latter had been out of the question, of course.

The job offer with Rocco's competitor had been, seemingly out of the blue, and a step down for her, but she hadn't dismissed it out of hand. The knowledge that Rocco would dislike the idea even more was why she'd kept the offer under wraps.

She sighed. 'I'd meant to tell you.'

'Really? When?' he sliced at her, derision rife in his tone. 'As you were walking out the door to my competition?'

'When I was sure I even wanted the job. Things were happening so fast. We were newly engaged and the Abu Dhabi project was about to take off and—'

'So you thought the best way forward was to give the opposition a lending hand?'

'No! If you must know, my professionalism was being called into question because…because we were involved. It didn't matter that we were engaged. Everyone thought I landed my position because I was bedding the boss. My degrees and hard work didn't count for anything, not when I apparently only needed to bat my eyelashes to get a promotion.' Humiliating heat suffused her face at the admission and the memory of the whispering campaign she'd tried to overlook, but which had become unbearable in the end. Unable to bear the force of his stare, she turned her head, only to have her move thwarted when strong fingers cupped her jaw and reversed her retreat.

His eyes had narrowed into icy slits. 'Who called your conduct into question?'

'It doesn't matter who.' The past was the past. The last thing she was going to do was name Rocco's cousin Alessandro as the prime culprit in her harassment and character assassination whenever the chance had arisen.

Alessandro Vitelli had pretended to be cordial with her in Rocco's presence, but hadn't bothered to hide his contempt when they had been alone.

The one time she'd confronted him and attempted to ascertain why he despised her so much, he'd implied it was all in her head. And had actually laughed at her.

Mia had tried to put that unpleasant episode behind her.

She'd seen the way Rocco fiercely protected his family, especially his grandmother. He wouldn't have welcomed her pointing fingers then and she had nothing to gain by pointing fingers now. 'You were so convinced I was in the wrong when you acted as judge, jury and executioner, and doled out your punishment. Why do you want to know anyway? Because there's a possibility you might have been wrong?' she threw at him, and added a sweet smile. 'If that's the case, then maybe I should leave you to wallow in your guilt.'

To say her response had annoyed him was an understatement. The hand that left her jaw to curve around her nape tightened only a split second before he yanked her close.

Her breath fled her lungs as the hands she threw up connected with hard muscles flexing beneath the expensive cotton of his shirt. Heat flared within her, igniting sensation along nerve endings now straining with acute excitement.

'Wh-what are you doing?' she gasped as he hauled her into his lap.

'Reminding myself that there must have been something besides your abrasive tongue I found so appealing about you three years ago.' His mouth hovered over hers, the hiss of his words landing like explosive little kisses on her lips.

With a desperate gasp, she parted them to suck in oxygen and trembled violently when a primitive growl echoed from his throat. One hand slid down her back to cup her behind, exerting pressure to bring her even closer.

'You…we can't—'

'I assure you, Mia, we can, and I fully intend to.'

His mouth breached that last centimetre, searing her own with a burning fire that immediately overwhelmed, consumed her so every thought, every single objection flew straight out of her head.

Salvation came in the form of a loud snuffle as Gianni stirred in his sleep.

Beneath her, Rocco stiffened at the sound, then

dropped his forehead to hers with a muted groan. 'I now know what parents mean when they bemoan their children killing their sex lives.' Warm self-derision invited her to share the joke.

'You can rest easy, Rocco. We don't have a sex life to bemoan. Hell, after we meet with your lawyers and get this straightened out, we don't even need to be in the same vicinity unless strictly necessary.'

Her voice was reassuringly firm and even, her spine straight.

But inside, Mia was trembling. Crumbling beneath the brooding, enigmatic look he sent her. Because that look was ten times more potent than the one he'd delivered that chilling day in his office when he'd annihilated her.

And as the limo sped towards London, her instincts shrieked that they were far from done. That she was nowhere near being free of Rocco Vitelli.

CHAPTER SIX

THE OFFICES OF ROCCO's lawyers were located exactly where Mia suspected they would be—slap bang in the middle of the Square Mile ensconced behind its towers of steel and glass.

Sharply suited professionals moved around with brisk efficiency. Within minutes, they were whisked skyward and into a sleek conference room. Gianni took it all in his stride, his eyes wide as he looked around him. His usually effervescent questions had quietened down, perhaps instinctively sensing the momentous occasion. Or it might have been the firm hold his father had on him, the awe with which her son looked up at his father as they were ushered into the conference room.

Mia didn't want to speculate any more than her wild imagination was already hammering at her. Rocco hadn't spoken to her since her tight announcement in the car following their horrid little entanglement. His calculating gaze had settled on her more than a few times though, enough to heighten the sense of unsettling dread bubbling beneath her skin. She refused to engage in whatever he was plotting behind those sharply intelligent eyes.

A few short hours. That was all she needed to hold it together before she could be back in Hampshire with her son. All further dealings after today would be through lawyers she could employ once she was back on her feet.

The door opened, and a stream of lawyers entered. It was easy to distinguish between the Italian contingent and their English counterparts. The Italians were more flamboyantly dressed, their bespoke Milan suits shrieking their Latin flair, while their English colleagues were a little more conservative, although both could not have been mistaken for anything other than the sharp pool of sharks Rocco retained.

Conservative greetings were exchanged, and Mia watched them align themselves across the conference table.

They were barely settled when Rocco leaned forward, his eyes fixed on the senior partner. 'Do you have answers for me?'

The older gentleman, with greying hair and rimless glasses, nodded. 'Our investigators are still working through how this debacle came to be but my team has been able to confirm that your earlier suspicions were right. The documentation is all fraudulent.'

A tight knot unfurled in Mia's belly, her breath expelling sharply. After years of living under the strain of persecution, she couldn't believe how completely she'd been duped. But the utmost emotion rolling through her was relief.

Slowly, though, bitterness followed. Things had gone seriously wrong but it still couldn't be denied that Rocco had cut her completely out of his life, not bothering to answer any of her emails long before this fraudulent court case had been brought.

'How?' she blurted, her voice thick with emotion she couldn't contain. 'How could this have been done without you or Rocco knowing?' Deep down she suspected she knew. Only someone with a vindictive agenda and in a position of trust could've done this. Someone with the backing of Vitelli billions.

The English lawyer turned to her. 'That was what we were hoping you would be able to shed some light on, Miss Gallagher.'

She frowned. 'Me?'

Another lawyer, this one an Italian, leaned forward. 'You attended the court, *sì*?' he asked, his accent thick as he peered at her.

She gritted her teeth, choosing not to rise to the clear scepticism in his tone. 'If you are in any way insinuating that I knew all of this was some huge set-up, you couldn't be more wrong.'

'The lawyers for the claimant are a small firm, we have discovered. Little more than a father and son outfit. The father, the one who dealt specifically with your case, is no longer practising. In fact he has fallen ill and is not in a position to testify to many of these allegations.'

Dismay hollowed her stomach. 'And his son?'

'Claims to have no knowledge of this affair.'

'That's terribly convenient, isn't it?' she snapped.

The lawyers exchanged glances. It was clear to Mia they had been thinking the same thing. *About her.*

She slapped her hands on the table. 'What exactly is going on here? I came here to clear my name. And you started off this meeting by confirming that these allegations are bogus. So why do I feel I'm still under suspicion?' She turned towards Rocco as she asked the last question. He was staring at her, narrow-eyed and speculative again. 'Rocco? What is this?'

He shrugged. 'We're all trying to find answers, *cara*.'

She hated that he used that soft endearment. It was dangerous and misleading. Hypnotic in a way that swayed her into overlooking the sharp eyes still brimming with suspicion. 'Well, I'm sorry, but I don't have any,' she remarked, bitter memory cutting sharply through her. 'I got the summons and I turned up at court and grasped enough to understand that I was being accused of harassing and stalking you.' Past hurt seared her insides but she refused to let it affect her. She needed to hold it together just enough to finish this and be gone. 'The lawyer I hired confirmed it too. You were clearly stated as the plaintiff. So this is all on you. It's your business to find out.'

'But you do know something, don't you?' Rocco said it again softly, his eyes boring into her.

'I'm not going to keep speculating. I've told you everything I know.'

'But not everything you *suspect*,' he pressed.

She kept her mouth mutinously shut.

His gaze remained on her face, probing beneath her skin for another minute before he faced his lawyers. 'Someone impersonated me and pulled this off without any of you knowing. I'm beginning to wonder why I keep you on retainer if this is the level of service I receive.'

Half a dozen lawyers shuffled their papers and

twitched in their seats. Eventually the senior partner spoke. 'While we don't wish to speculate, Mr Vitelli, we all agree that it could only have been someone close to you, someone who was sure they could carry this out without suspicion.' A few glances settled on her.

Mia stiffened, ready to launch another defence but Rocco beat her to it. 'Someone close to me?' he echoed, his face taut.

The lawyer shifted in his seat before nodding. 'Your investigators have been in touch with your IT department. It seems there's evidence of deleted emails and possible tampering with your server. We think that the only person who could have done that may have been your assistant.'

Rocco's jaw clenched. 'My assistant has been with me since the very beginning. I trust him with my life. It's not him. Look for a different culprit.'

Gianpaolo, Rocco's assistant, had come straight from university into his role. Even Mia knew he would cut off his own arm before he betrayed Rocco. Just as she knew Rocco's implicit trust in his assistant, where he'd had none for her, bruised deep.

Silence descended on the table, only disturbed when Gianni rose from his seat, reaching for the pen in front of Rocco. He'd been well-behaved thus far but Mia knew restlessness was about to set in with a vengeance. 'Are we done here? I need to tend to my son.'

'Pardon me, Miss Gallagher, I have one question. It may be a little bit indelicate, but it needs to be asked. Did you make any enemies while you were working at Vitelli Construction?'

She barely stopped herself from glancing at Rocco,

the man who'd made himself public and private enemy number one the moment she'd attended an meeting with his competitor, then compounded her sins by informing him she wasn't ready to start a family on his schedule. She bit her tongue, a part of her unwilling to antagonise the situation and a part of her wanting to state blatantly that he was the only nemesis she could think of.

But then he wasn't the only one, was he?

Alessandro Vitelli had made it his life's mission to make hers miserable the moment she'd set foot in Vitelli Construction. Could she say it now? It had been established that she had been duped. Wasn't that enough?

'If you know who it is, Mia, spit it out,' Rocco said tightly, his face taut as he stared at her.

She inhaled slowly, her instinct screaming at her to keep the information to herself. But at the same time she wanted the truth of her suspicions explored. Deep down she knew she couldn't rest until she discovered who had done this to her. 'The only person I can think of is your cousin Alessandro.'

The first expression of shock was Rocco's sharp intake of breath. Then the Italian contingent exchanged glances before their faces tightened.

Mia held herself tight. 'What? You asked me a question and I'm sorry if you don't like the answer.'

'You happened to pick the only person who wouldn't be able to corroborate your statement. A little curious, don't you think?' Rocco replied. If he had been tense a moment ago, he was downright rigid now.

'What are you talking about? Why wouldn't he?'

Brackets formed around his lips as he tightened them, staring at her for another tense moment before he rasped, 'You know exactly what I mean. You accuse a dead man incapable of telling his part of whatever story you're concocting.'

A cold rush of dread unravelled through her. Partly because she was receiving evidence that Rocco didn't truly believe her. The other was at the news he'd just delivered. 'Alessandro is dead?' she whispered.

Again his lips flattened. 'His car crash was sensationalised by the papers.' His tone of voice suggested that she should know.

'I don't keep abreast of news headlines. Especially foreign ones. I'm too busy looking after my son.'

'The TV and newspapers carried the story for days. It would have been impossible to miss.'

'Well, I'm telling you it is possible because I missed it. The question remains do you believe me or do you think I'm making this up as well?'

'What reason would he have to do this?' Rocco asked stiffly.

She forced a shrug. 'That's what you have to find out for yourself.'

His nostrils flared, a very Latin, very emotive expression that sent a shiver down her spine.

'So we have a perpetrator who is no longer with us and a co-conspirator lawyer who is unable to testify as to his role in this?' He gave a thin smile.

She answered with one of her own. 'Life has a funny way of unravelling, doesn't it?'

His narrowed gaze raked her face before he turned his attention back to his lawyers. 'We keep investigating. We don't stop searching until we know the facts for certain. Is that understood?'

Brisk nods accompanied verbal assurances.

Rocco rose, leaned down to place a gentle hand on Gianni's head, attracting his son's attention from the picture he'd been drawing on the piece of paper.

Gianni looked set to protest at the interruption. Anticipating it, Rocco murmured in his ear. With a pleased grin, Gianni grabbed the paper and pen and jumped to his feet. Without addressing his lawyers again, Rocco strode after his son, leaving Mia to follow.

In the lift, Gianni chatted on, negating the need for his parents to converse. But the look Rocco pinned on her announced loud and clear that the conversation was far from over. Mia dragged her gaze from his, so overwrought by the events of the last hour that, once they were in the car, it took a while to notice that the driver was heading back out of London.

She turned to Rocco, who was staring at her, one finger dragging slowly across his lower lip in that contemplative way she knew all too well.

The question she'd intended to ask about where they were going dried in her throat. 'When did he die?'

He exhaled heavily. 'Almost eighteen months ago,' he replied.

'Was he…is his family okay?'

'He was alone in the car, if that's what you're asking. Allegra and the kids were at home in Palermo.'

'Where did it happen?'

'He was on a business trip to Brazil when it happened. He lost control of his sports car.'

Her heart twisted. 'I… I'm sorry for your loss. I know you two were close.'

He nodded briefly, his eyes flashing with something

akin to pain before he expunged it. 'You really expect me to believe Alessandro did this to you? What would have been his motive?' The questions were sharp, rife with suspicion.

She shrugged. 'He didn't like me, Rocco. And that's not a frivolous or desperate observation I'm casting around because I've no one else to pin this on, if you think that's what I'm trying to do. Alessandro actively despised me for whatever reason. He didn't want me in the company and he certainly didn't want me to marry into the illustrious Vitelli family.'

His features darkened, thunder rolling across his forehead as he stared at her. 'We were together for two years. You never bothered to tell me any of this?'

Again she shrugged. 'Maybe I was trying to spare your feelings. Or maybe I was misguided enough to think I might be able to win him over eventually with my sparkling personality. What does it matter? You'll only make up your mind one way or the other, won't you? Why am I even wasting my breath with this?'

'Because you spoke his name in the boardroom. And I'd like to think that you wouldn't speak so ill of the dead.'

Frustration rushed through her. 'We're simply going around in circles. Until we know exactly who did this, there's no point speculating, is there? So can we be done for now?' She stared at the window and then returned her attention to him. 'Where are we going?'

'To my house in Knightsbridge.'

Her eyes widened in surprise. 'I didn't know you had a house in England.'

A brittle smile ghosted his lips then just as quickly

disappeared. 'It was meant to be a surprise wedding gift. For you.'

Her heart lurched. She steeled herself against it, determined not to dwell on silly might-have-beens. 'Why did you keep it?'

He gave a careless shrug. 'I leave my real estate portfolio to my advisors. If it'd been prudent for them to dispose of it, they would've, I'm sure.'

The dismissive comment was meant to sting. And it did. Mia steeled herself harder. 'Well, I thought I'll be returning to Hampshire.'

His gaze flicked to Gianni. 'You think our son will appreciate being cooped up in the car for another several hours?'

She answered reluctantly. 'No. Frankly, I'm surprised he's been this calm.'

'*Bene*, we'll stop in Knightsbridge. I've arranged for us to have lunch. We have further things to discuss before any of this is resolved.'

'Like what?'

He raised an eyebrow. 'Have you forgotten there is still the matter of your employment to discuss?'

'My employment?' she echoed, disregarding the electric cluster that formed in her stomach. 'If you think I'm taking a job with you, you are very much mistaken.'

Hard amusement lit his eyes. 'Perhaps you should wait until it's offered before you refuse.'

She shook her head, unwilling to even accommodate the idea. Her last mistake of mixing business with pleasure had ended disastrously. So much so even the idea of just business with Rocco was unfathomable to her. 'My future employment is none of your business.

All I want is for my name to be cleared so I can get on with my life.'

'And we will discuss how to facilitate that during lunch.'

She knew she was being manipulated but, short of insisting on being returned home, she had no choice.

'We'll come with you. But I'm catching the train this afternoon, once we're done.' She didn't intend to stay in Rocco's company any longer than was necessary.

'We'll see,' he said, another enigmatic smile ghosting his lips before he turned his attention to his phone.

For the rest of the journey, Rocco conducted several conversations in rapid-fire Italian, which she wasn't quick enough to grasp save for establishing they were all business calls.

Twenty-five minutes later they pulled up in front of a stunning house in a tree-lined avenue in Knightsbridge. Mia was vaguely cognisant of house prices, enough to know that the dwelling they stopped in front of was well into double figures in millions.

It was set over three stories with a grey slate roof, the pristine white exterior gleaming with a rarefied air of class and timeless elegance that the whole neighbourhood clung to.

Confronted by the heavy white oak door, Mia was suddenly reluctant to enter. She didn't want to know what her life might have been like if Rocco, and circumstances, hadn't worked against her.

If she hadn't taken that meeting.

If someone, likely Alessandro, hadn't perpetrated such cruelty on her.

If she hadn't asked Rocco about his London property ten minutes ago!

But she couldn't change any of it. So she sucked in a breath, and entered the house that Rocco claimed would've been hers had they married. All the while conscious of his sharp, unwavering scrutiny.

As she'd suspected, the interior was breathtaking.

Polished marble floors gleamed, reflecting lofty ceilings and crown mouldings. Stunning chandeliers and strategically placed lights spotlighted tasteful *objets d'art* in the entry hallway.

In the living room, bespoke white furniture with warm accessories were arranged just the way she would have done it, given the chance. But it was the white grand piano taking up pride of place at the far side of the room, with a wall of paintings behind it, that stopped Mia in her tracks.

She knew each painting by heart, having rhapsodised over her favourite English painter to Rocco over many stimulating art and cultural conversations. Just as she'd expressed the desire to learn to play piano at some distant point in her future.

She whirled towards him and encountered his expectant, *mocking* expression. Her lips moved, but no words emerged.

Asking him if he'd deliberately brought her here to rub her face in what she could've been would only invite further hurt. Not to mention be far too revealing.

'Nothing to say?' he invited when a terse minute passed.

She turned away without answering, her gaze rushing over the rest of the space, awed but not surprised that Rocco's steel trap of a mind had stored away bits and pieces of her dream home wish list and effortlessly replicated it.

Sternly, she pulled her gaze from admiring the beautiful interior; reminded herself that she wasn't here to gawp at the stunning paintings or the interior design plucked straight from her heart. She was here to finalise the next step of her life. A life that had been cruelly and ruthlessly halted by this man, who now leaned against the doorway, gazing at her as if he owned every cell in her body.

'Shall we get on with this?'

'So impatient,' he commented, a smirk playing around his lips. 'You haven't even mentioned what you think of the house.'

Her shoulder felt leaden as she shrugged. 'It'll make a gorgeous home for someone once you get bored of it, I'm sure.'

His mocking expression evaporated and his jaw clenched once but Mia didn't congratulate herself on landing the blow. Not when her insides were clenched tight with the need to hold herself together.

'Perhaps I'll hang onto it, set down roots for Gianni. He's half English, after all,' he drawled.

'Are we really discussing real estate? I would've thought you'd be upset by the events of the last few hours.'

He lifted one masculine shoulder, drawing her attention to the sheer breadth and magnificence of his towering body. 'I'm learning not to sweat the details. My investigators will uncover the truth in due time.'

'You're just prepared to shrug it off until it all comes together for you?'

'What's the point of stressing about it? Like you're so eager to, we need to get on with other discussions. But first things first.' He strolled over to a console table, lifted the phone and spoke in Italian. Almost immediately, Mia heard the click of approaching footsteps.

The middle-aged woman who entered the room was conservatively dressed, and pleasant-looking. She greeted Rocco before glancing at her.

'This is my Mrs Simpson, my housekeeper,' Rocco introduced. 'She's already prepared Gianni's lunch.'

The older woman smiled at Mia. 'I have three grandchildren of my own so I know just what a two-year-old likes to eat. It's all set up in the kitchen. If you don't mind him coming with me?'

To respond any other way would have been discourteous. So Mia nodded. 'Thank you. If you need me, I'll be…' She paused, glancing at Rocco.

'We'll be in the dining room, having our own lunch. But Gianni is going to be a good boy for Mrs Simpson, aren't you, *mio figlio*?'

Gianni, who had looked up from his drawing with interest when the housekeeper entered, nodded at his father. She'd been concerned about how her son would take to having a male figure in his life. Judging from the look that passed between father and son, he was coping brilliantly. A part of her wanted to be disappointed but it was a small, selfish part that she managed to smother as Mrs Simpson and Gianni walked away, hand in hand.

'He's only going to the other room, Mia, not Outer Mongolia,' Rocco quipped.

She sent him a sharp look. 'I'm not used to other people taking care of him, okay?'

He regarded her steadily. 'I'm becoming aware of that. I recall you disliked talking about your family. Do I assume hiding away in your little village was by choice?'

'If by choice you mean was I alone once my grand-mother passed away soon after Gianni was born, then yes.'

His eyes shadowed. 'Were you close?'

A swell of sadness filled her heart. 'Close enough to make me regret not spending more time with her,' she said before she could trap the revealing words.

'Meaning?' Rocco pressed.

'Meaning we all have regrets. Less time with my grandmother is one of mine.'

His gaze probed. Deep. Making his next words un-expected. *'Le mie condoglianze.'*

Condolences.

'Thank you.'

He nodded. 'But things are going to change. You know that, don't you?'

She raised her chin, unwilling to divulge that she suspected the very same thing. 'Do I?'

'Sì, cara,' he said far too softly, ambling to a halt in front of her. For an eternity, he stared down at her, then lifted a finger and traced it down her cheek. 'For start-ers, you are no longer alone.'

The words echoed through her, sinking into un-guarded spaces inside her, awing and terrifying in equal measure. She tried to read his face, but Rocco gave nothing away.

'Come.' He held out his hand, his command softer but imperious.

The urge to take his proffered hand was far too tempting. So she refused it, and walked past him. Only to stop when she got to the door, having no clue where the dining room was. Still she forced herself not to look at him, not to be overwhelmed all over again by the ever-morphing Rocco, who seemed to have changed from ruthless strategist in the car to something bordering on…charming?

'This way,' he said when he joined her, directing her down a short hallway and into another opulently appointed room with a long, antique dining table she was willing to bet had belonged to a prince or a lofty aristocrat once upon its lifetime.

At the top of the table, an elaborate setting for two was arranged with gleaming silver and crystal ware.

Rocco pulled out a chair, saw her seated and took his own seat. In silence, he uncovered dishes and served her before indicating the wine resting in the sterling silver ice bucket.

'Would you like some wine? Or are you…?' He paused, an almost bashful look on his face as his gaze dropped to her chest. 'You are not still breastfeeding, are you?' he asked, his voice curiously husky.

She spluttered, an unwilling laugh rising in her throat before she could stop it. 'Gianni's two and half years old, Rocco.'

His gaze lingered for another heated second on her breasts before he shrugged, a wry smile curving his lips. 'I'm still learning, *cara*. So is that a yes to wine?' he drawled.

She needed to keep a clear head for what was coming. But what harm would a small, confidence-bolstering glass do? 'A small one, thanks.'

He poured a half-glass for her and then filled his. The first bite of poached salmon was heavenly, but anxiety over the upcoming discussion eventually killed her enjoyment of the meal. After a few minutes of pushing it around her plate, she looked up, noting that Rocco was equally uninterested in his food.

Almost in accordance, they gave up pretence of eating and sat back. When the silence stretched, she folded her napkin and dropped it next to her plate. 'We need to discuss next steps.'

'Agreed.'

'So?' she pressed when he didn't elaborate.

'So, you're not returning to Hampshire, Mia.'

'Maybe not right this minute, but I'm definitely...' She stopped when he gave a brisk shake of his head.

'No. To get what you want you need to give me what I want and neither of those scenarios involve you returning to the back end of nowhere. I think we need to agree on that before we go forward.'

CHAPTER SEVEN

ONCE UPON A time when she'd dreamed of being exonerated of these fraudulent charges, she'd imagined a scene when Rocco would grovel at her feet, beg her forgiveness for all the wrong perpetrated against her. Over time that dream had morphed, reality throwing harsh light on that fairy tale, reminding her of the ruthless being she was spinning whimsical webs around.

In the much more realistic scenario, Rocco had perhaps thrown a brusque apology her way for the treatment she'd suffered, perhaps even tossing lawyers at her, tasked with providing adequate compensation to ensure she kept her mouth shut, but ultimately Rocco had walked away, shrugging his mile-wide shoulders as if nothing besides a pesky irritation had occurred.

Nowhere in those scenarios had she accommodated sitting down to lunch as a prelude to negotiating a deal with him. 'You want me to give you more than I already have? You don't think what you've put me through is enough?'

For one blazing second, raw emotion flashed across his face. 'What was done to you was deplorable, regardless of who perpetrated it. For that you have my regret.

Mi dispiace.' He spread his hands in a typically Latin gesture she couldn't help but follow before she could rein in her composure.

He was sorry.

It wasn't the grovelling she'd dreamed of, but it was…enough to ease something inside her.

'You will get the chance to name your price and necessary reparations will be made.'

That soft place hardened, ejecting a bitter snort. 'This all sounds like a business transaction to you, doesn't it?'

Another flash of emotion threw doubt on her assertion. 'You forget that I suffered by this course of action too,' he said, his voice a rough rasp.

Her heart lurched for a foolish moment, before she registered that he was talking about Gianni. Not her.

Never her.

'If you would hear me out, perhaps my solution might salve your feelings of…hurt?'

'Nothing will repair what I've endured. Right now, I just want move on. Forget it, and *you*, ever happened.'

His eyes roved lazily over her face, clocking her agitated breathing before he leaned forward. 'It was never going to be as simple as stating your case, wrapping this up, and walking away, Mia. Surely you knew that?'

'You keep implying that I owe you something. Let's get things straight between us. I owe you nothing.'

He eased back in his chair, but Mia wasn't fooled for a moment. Tension coiled within him, the barely bridled domination emanating from him all but screaming at her that he intended to win this argument. Whatever it might be.

'What about Gianni, Mia? You told me three years

ago that you didn't intend to have children. So you'll excuse me if I find all of this new, devoted-to-motherhood part of you a little bit surprising?'

She gasped, felt the blood drain from her head as she stared at him. 'You think I'm faking it?'

'Are you?'

'How dare you!' She whirled around, heading blindly for the door with one intention in mind—to claim her child and leave this place.

'What do you think you're doing?'

'Whatever the hell I want. And right now the thing I want the most in this world is to never see your face again. I'm going to get my son and we're leaving.'

'Calm yourself, Mia. You really want Gianni to see you in this state?'

She reversed direction, her emotions boiling as she faced him. 'You're unbelievable, do you know that? Now you're accusing me of upsetting my son?'

He spread his arms again, his eyes narrowing as he approached. 'Don't put words in my mouth, *cara*. From what I've seen so far, you're devoted to our child.'

Again, his unexpected words weakened the hard knot in her chest. But she knew better than to trust it. 'Thank you, but I sense a *but* in there.'

'But this display of…emotion serves no purpose. Like I said before, you have cared for Gianni alone but it doesn't need to be the case going forward. You can deal with me now or you can deal with my lawyers before you reach the home you are so determined to run back to. Which is it to be?'

She inhaled sharply, surprised at herself for momentarily forgetting the depths Rocco could sink to to achieve what he wanted. 'You haven't changed even a little bit, have you?'

His resolve was a hard, unshakeable mask. 'I discover a son I never knew existed and you expect me to do what exactly, Mia? Go back to Palermo and forget all about him? Or were you hoping I'd sit back and let you dictate terms? When have you known me to be that… *unaffected* when it comes to something I truly want?' he asked, his voice deceptive lazily.

Since the question was rhetorical, and since the throb of something in his tone tossed her back to another time frame, when that something he'd wanted was *her*, she kept her answer locked in her throat.

While the net tightened around her, dragging her towards a precarious destination she didn't want to go. Still, she managed to raise her chin, look him square in the eyes. 'I'll give you ten minutes to hear you out. But I won't be railroaded into anything, just so we're clear,' she stated, pleased when her voice came out even, without hinting at the hysteria bubbling beneath her skin. 'What do you want? Specifically?'

He didn't answer immediately. He stared at her, gauging the emotions she was grappling with before his gaze sauntered down her body to her toes. The return was slow and hot, setting off fireworks she didn't want to acknowledge. 'A few things come to mind. But for now, specifically, my presence in my son's life. And I suspect the way to achieve that is to give you what you most want.'

What she most wanted was to remove herself from his orbit. To stop the fizzle of giddy static from lighting her veins every time her eyes met his. Every time she breathed him in. 'And what do you think that is?'

'Why, a return to the career status you enjoyed before our parting, of course. Am I wrong?' he enquired, a knowing gleam in his eyes she wanted to erase but knew she couldn't. Because she *did* want back what she'd lost.

'I'll get it back. But it'll be on my own, with no handout from you, thank you very much. If you think that's some sort of carrot to dangle to get what you want, then the answer is no. My son isn't some bartering chip for you to trade,' she stated.

'So much righteous pride,' he drawled. 'Are you sure you're wise to dismiss my help?'

'Help? When it comes with an endless amount of strings? No, thanks,' she reiterated. The voice that urged her to stop talking grew louder. Even if she intended to reclaim her life by herself, did she want to brazenly antagonise him? She'd been out of the workforce for the better part of three years. Did she really want to start at the bottom of the pile again when a few words from Rocco could pave the way for a decent enough re-entry, enabling her to look after herself and Gianni? Wasn't it the least he owed her?

As if he knew the direction of her thoughts, he stepped closer, bringing the full force of his aura and the temptation of his body within mouth-watering reach. 'Is that your definitive answer, then, *cara*? Your decision-making used to be so prudent and pragmatic. It was one of the things I admired about you. Have you grown rusty or are you simply disregarding what your brain is telling you simply to continue tussling with me?'

She wanted to protest, toss out some clever answer

that would put him in his place once and for all, but the voice urging caution held her tongue for the moment.

He continued, his voice turning lower and deeper, almost seductive as he laid his plans before her. 'Let me tell you what my intentions are while you think about the wisdom of contemptuously dismissing me out of hand. I'm not sure whether you've kept up with Vitelli Construction's progress in the last few years?' One eyebrow tilted, as he waited a beat for her to answer. When she didn't give him the satisfaction of confessing the secret compulsion she'd had of tracking his company's stellar progress over the years, he carried on.

'Our Middle East expansion has now reached eight countries. The workforce is five times the size of what it was when you were last with me. Before his passing, Alessandro also expanded the Latin American arm. Eventually, should you wish it, you can take a pick of where you wish to base yourself.'

Her heart jumped, a treacherous little action she condemned. Because she didn't want to be seduced by what he was offering. Didn't want to be tempted by memories of working alongside him, basking in the glow of his intelligent mind and the thrill of knowing she was working for the best of the best, her career poised to soar as a result of her hard work.

She managed to throttle down the unwelcome excitement, and clinically sieved through his words. 'Eventually,' she echoed. 'What exactly do you mean by *eventually*?'

Incisive eyes rested on her face, dropped down to her mouth before rising to meet her gaze. He shrugged, walked past her to shut the doors of the dining room.

Foreboding rained icy shivers down her spine, but she clenched her fist, forced herself to hold her ground as he sauntered back towards her. 'I'm assuming you wish to be where our son is, don't you?'

She frowned. 'Is that even a serious question? Of course I do.'

He nodded, as if she had given him the exact answer he wanted. 'Then we're agreed.'

Her ire and confusion intensified. 'What exactly are we agreed on?'

'That where I am, you will be. With our son. To start off with, that place will be in Palermo. For the next six months at least. Perhaps even a year. Depending on Nonna's health issues and how quickly she recovers.'

She spluttered, unsure which outrage to address first. 'You think I'm coming to Italy to live with you? Why on earth would I do that?'

When you threw me out. When for weeks every street I walked in Palermo reminded me of you and what I'd lost.

His steady regard didn't falter. 'What other solution do you propose? That I commute every other day to your little Hampshire hamlet? With Nonna living in a faceless motel somewhere close by, perhaps?'

'Where you or your grandmother live has nothing to do with me. I'm not going anywhere with you. Let's make that absolutely clear.'

'Then how do you propose we raise our son to-gether?' he delivered with a deceptively silky voice.

Raise our son together.

Against her better judgement, those four words sent a treacherous rush through her. Reminded her of everything she'd yearned for when she'd tried to give him the news of her pregnancy. A chance to raise their child together. A chance to rewrite her own history through Gianni. To give him what her own mother had failed to give her.

A relationship with her father. For her son not to be tormented as she had been with questions about the man whose name appeared on her birth certificate but who she'd never clapped eyes on because her mother refused point-blank to discuss him, save for the fact that he was a mistake that should never have happened.

Much like Mia had been to her.

As if he knew how much the words affected her, Rocco strode closer, his eyes not leaving her face. 'Tell me about your father, Mia.'

She stiffened, more against the anguish of discussing the man she didn't know than by Rocco's question. 'Why?'

'Because, as we're both discovering, we were engaged for a time over three years ago, but clearly didn't know a few important details about one another.'

'And why do you think that is?'

He shrugged. 'Perhaps we thought we'd have time to uncover what needed uncovering.'

'Do you think so? Or were we too afraid to find out we wouldn't like what we discovered beneath the surface so avoided it?'

It was his turn to stiffen. 'Perhaps. So, let's be brave now. Let's stop the speculation,' he said, cleverly tossing the ball back in her court.

Her father.

Her answer was simple. And soul-destroying. 'I don't

know a thing about him because I've never met him. My mother refused to tell me who he was or what happened between them. Other than he was a mistake she'd rather forget ever existed.'

Mia knew by revealing that, she was exposing her jugular. Or at the very least, giving him ammunition for his argument. But Rocco's gaze gentled, his breath slowly releasing as he absorbed her words. 'You may think it a bad thing that your mother withheld details from you. But perhaps she was protecting you. Maybe you were better off remaining oblivious.'

Memories of her mother's bitterness whenever Mia had asked about her father made her think otherwise. 'Would you have let it go were you in my shoes?'

His lips curved in a rueful smile. '*Assolutamente no.* Even if it meant discovering that one's parents were far...worth revering.'

Her eyes widened, the notion that Rocco was offering her a brief glimpse behind his private, emotional veil stopping her breath.

They regarded each other for an endless stretch before, with a conscious shuttering of his emotions, he continued, 'Despite opposing forces, circumstance has brought my son and I together. I don't intend to squander that chance.'

Still a little shaken and more than curious at his revelation, she took a moment to gather her wits. 'I didn't intend to throw Gianni into the deep end of the relationship-with-family pool by uprooting him to Italy.'

'And *I* will not be sidelined to part-time parenthood. Gianni is mine. You will give me the chance to get to know him as I haven't been able since his birth.'

'And what I want and what's best for Gianni doesn't matter?'

The shrewd gleam in his eyes said he had the answer to that too. 'You disagree that what's best for Gianni is to be with both his mother *and* father?'

'Of course not,' she bristled.

'Then it helps immensely that I know *you* love Italy. Almost as much as I do.'

She had, once upon a time. Had uprooted her life for him and blissfully contemplated becoming an Italian citizen after they were married without a single regret. She'd never really got around to learning Italian because their work had been based mostly in the Middle East, but she'd loved everything about Italy and had looked forward to spending the rest of her life there with him. How stupid she'd been. And now he was proposing she go back to where he had dismantled her whole life?

No way was that happening.

'That was a long time ago. I've made a life for myself and Gianni in England and I intend to keep on living here.'

'Answer me this, Mia. Why did you go to the trouble to contact me three years ago if you didn't want me to play a part in our child's life?' he asked 'Was it because you didn't want to revisit what happened to you with your own father on our son?'

A cold, heavy stone settled in her belly. And she couldn't even blame him for cleverly using her history against her. Because it was the truth.

Her own loneliness and abandonment issues had been acute and painful, a past she carried with her as a reminder to not let her own child endure the pain she'd suffered. And yes, she had hoped in some secret part of her that Rocco, learning of the child she carried, would rethink his absolute rejection of her, let her back into his life.

But that was before the scales had fallen from her eyes. That was before she'd fathomed the depths of his ruthlessness. Who was to say that this wasn't another calculated scheme on his part to lure her into his web?

'Well?' he pushed.

She looked deeper into his eyes, unable to remain unaffected by the turbulent gleam that suggested this was important to him. 'For good or ill, I believe every child has the right to know his parents.' Before the turbulence turned into triumph, she rushed on, 'But expecting me to blithely step back in time and pick up where we left off...' She tailed off when his eyes conducted that heated exploration again, stripping her of every ounce of composure.

'Perhaps not pick up exactly where we left off, but I don't see why some things can't go back to the way they were.'

'Whatever you're implying, I suggest you stop.' She'd intended to snap her response. Only it emerged uneven, detonated by that vicious thrill of excitement that simply refused to die. The memory of the torrid kiss in the car kept pushing to the front of her thoughts, reminding her of his skill as a lover, the insatiable depths of his passion, and her eager acceptance of everything he had to give.

Heat bloomed in her belly as he watched her with that knowing look. The one that mocked her every attempt at keeping cool, calm and collected.

'You can have your old position back,' he murmured, his voice deep and low and tempting enough to make her believe he was the devil himself, handing Eve the doomed apple.

Her heart lurched, thumping hard against her ribs.

He waited, watchful, taunting her with the knowledge that she was tempted. Oh, so tempted. She knew he wanted her to ask which position he was referring to, the subtle double entendre simply waiting to catch her out.

After a moment, where she battled against the drowning sensation, he added, 'Think of how much easier your life would be if you had it all back. How difficult things could get if you have to start from scratch. Is that what you really want, Mia?' he taunted softly, dangerously.

'Is that what this all boils down to? You threatening to withhold restoring my reputation if I don't agree to come to Palermo?'

His jaw gritted for a moment. 'You were an asset in my company before you decided to defect. Provided your skills haven't grown rusty, I could use someone with your expertise.'

'I didn't defect,' she snapped.

He didn't acknowledge her denial with so much as a blink. 'I don't need to threaten you. Contingent upon a few things, you can have your old position back.' He snapped his fingers. 'Just like that.'

'Contingent upon what?'

'The only reason I'll let you back is if you agree that you and I will be working very closely together. Where I can keep an eye on you. You will not be left to your own devices.'

'Next you'll be suggesting I wear an ankle monitor like a common criminal.'

His lips twisted with genuine amusement. 'Not an offer I'd have thought of myself. Thanks for the suggestion but maybe not. I don't think it's a good look for Vitelli Construction.'

'You find all of this funny, do you?'

A layer of humour left his face. 'I'm attempting to repair the damage done to you by giving you back everything you lost with all its advantages, and more. I suggest you stop fighting me on every angle before I withdraw the offer.'

She lifted her chin, snatching in short breaths so she wouldn't breathe in his intoxicating scent. 'You've listed what you think I want but have *you* stopped to ask yourself whether you want this? You've known Gianni for a mere twenty-four hours. How do I know you won't get bored a month from now?'

Affront, and some dark, anguished shadow she couldn't quite name, drenched his features. 'Because he's not some accessory I intend to toy with and toss away when the novelty wears off. Make no mistake, Mia. I want my son. And I mean full access. I want him embraced by his family, in Italy, where he belongs. For my grandmother not to fret over it and further damage her health. What I want is for those things to happen immediately and to stay that way for as long as possible until I deem it otherwise.'

She tilted her head, attempting to emulate his earlier humour. 'Are you sure you wouldn't prefer the ankle monitor? Because that sounds suspiciously like a prison sentence to me.'

He didn't return her amusement. 'Hardly, *cara*. I'm offering you everything you claimed you wanted when we were together three years ago. All I need from you is your agreement to live under my roof.'

'Live under your roof?' she echoed.

He stepped closer, until every corner of her vision was filled with him, her every sense infused with that illicit thrill he never failed to evoke in her, even when she knew deep in her bones that this kind of exposure was detrimental to her sanity. 'Not just live under my roof, *cara*. You will do all the above, after you take my name. In short, Mia, I want you to marry me. Accept my marriage proposal or there is no deal.'

CHAPTER EIGHT

ROCCO WASN'T SURE whether to be insulted or amused when a look of horror chased across her face.

'You want me to…to *marry* you?'

'*Sì.*'

She grew paler, and the last trace of amusement departed.

Watching closely, he could've sworn she swayed beneath the heavy demand of his words. For a single, unbridled moment, Rocco wanted her to exhibit more emotion, perhaps something resembling the naked rapture that'd accompanied her ecstatic *yes* when he'd asked this very same question three years ago. Even the somewhat unnerving *happy tears* he'd dabbed away then, he would've tolerated now.

Anything but the pale apprehension she was showing so far.

'Absolutely not.'

'Which part of it do you disagree with, considering it was what you agreed to three years ago, minus the blessing of our son, of course?'

'Oh, but you forget, I wasn't in the position where I knew your true colours, was I? That enlightening moment came later. Thankfully before I made the mistake you're suggesting I make again.'

A hard stone settled in his stomach. 'You believe marriage to me would've been a mistake?'

'When you're so quick to believe the worst about me? Yes!'

He dragged in a slow breath, attempting to calm the frenzied emotion that threatened to spin out of control whenever he was within arm's reach of this woman. 'Let's spell things out between us, then, so there's no misunderstanding this time around. This isn't a love match or some lofty declaration of devotion. This is simply a transaction. You regain your position in my company. I get my son under my roof and my grand-mother's health and well-being ensured.'

'And if I say no?'

'What is so wrong with attempting to strive for bet-ter where our son is concerned, Mia?'

'I...what?'

'Trust your instincts. Do you believe Gianni will come to any harm by being under my care?'

Her lashes swept down, veiling her expression from him. He shoved his hands in his pockets to prevent him from cupping her chin, tilting her gaze to his so he could read what she was hiding from him. 'No,' she murmured after an eternity.

His breath expelled in relief. 'Then, is what I'm pro-posing so bad?' he attempted to reason, although a very primitive, very masculine part of him simply wanted to throw her over his shoulder, find a dark cave to seal them both in to hash this out.

He clenched his gut against the sensation. It wasn't

one he particularly liked about himself but…hadn't he experienced this…primitive possessiveness with Mia from the very time he'd spotted her? This need for exclusivity with her where he'd neither cared nor accommodated that in any of his previous liaisons?

'Mia?' His voice was hoarser, sharper than he'd intended.

She startled, looked into his eyes and he realised, just like yesterday, she'd been equally caught up in carnal memory. A little too pleased with that knowledge, he raised an eyebrow, watched her flush before she averted her gaze.

'Don't overthink this. You, me and Gianni. Together. We all get what we want. You also make an old woman you claimed to like immeasurably happy. Is that so bad?'

Her soft lips twisted. 'You appeal to my better nature in the same breath you insult me. I never *claimed* to like your grandmother. I did.'

'Then why break her heart by denying her whatever time she has left with her great-grandchild?'

She paled again and he felt another bite of guilt. 'Whatever time she has left? Is she…ill?'

'I told you she collapsed when she saw Gianni's billboard. She hadn't been too well before that. Her doctors think it's her heart.'

She bit her lip, drawing Rocco's attention to the plump curve he longed to taste one more time. And several times after that. 'This is emotional blackmail.'

He firmed his resolve. 'It's the plain truth. I won't allow her to suffer further. Not if I can help it.'

Her gaze shifted to the door. 'I need time…to think.'

'What's there to think about? Don't you want your *career* back?' He couldn't stop himself from sneering the word. From emphasising the only thing she'd cared about when she was with him. 'You could be at your old desk in Milan as early as Monday morning.'

She inhaled sharply. 'You think that's all that matters to me. It's not. Not now I've Gianni to think about. We've never been apart and… I…'

'My grandmother and every member of my household will be devoted to his care when you're at work. Since Alessandro passed, Allegra and her children have moved into the villa. Gianni won't lack for anything.'

Another shadow passed across her face. 'Allegra and her children live with you?'

He nodded, eyes narrowed at her carefully neutral tone. 'Is that a problem?'

Long lashes swept down again. 'No, of course not. Besides, it's your house.'

'It'll be *our* house, when you accept my proposal.'

She swallowed, her eyes still not meeting his. Rocco wanted to ask why she was refusing him when most women within his social circle would turn cartwheels at the thought of bagging a man of his stature.

'Why marriage? It's not like you need a shotgun wedding to protect my honour or anything like that. Besides, you're already listed on Gianni's birth certificate as his father. Isn't that enough?'

He finally gave into the insane urge and closed the gap between them. He slid his hand along her jaw to cup her nape. He revelled in the slight shiver that raked her frame. 'It wasn't enough for you, Mia, and it's most definitely not enough for me. My parents abandoned

me when I was a child. Had it not been for Nonna's un-
flinching intervention, who knows where I would've
ended up? She gave up a better life for me. She almost
lost everything in the process. I won't deny her this.
Most importantly, I won't deny myself.'

The depth of the words he hadn't spoken to anyone else spilling from his lips shocked him. Perhaps he
wanted to reach someone who didn't exist. The woman
he'd thought shared his values when he'd placed his ring
on her finger three years ago. Whatever. They were
said and he couldn't take them back. Nor could he look
away from the wide-eyed shock in her own eyes as she
stared up him.

They stayed locked in that revealing little bubble. Not
breathing. Not speaking. The only movement his thumb
slowly tracing back and forth across her lower lip.

But eventually, that seemingly unquenching well of
lust swelled, ebbing and flowing in stronger waves that
threatened to consume them. A soft sound, which he
deciphered as a moan a few seconds later, rippled the
air between them.

As he'd yearned her to, she swayed into him, her lips
parting, her warm breath caressing his thumb, sending
a stronger wave of electricity through his body.

Rocco leaned down, unable to stem the tide con-
suming him.

A hair's breadth away from tasting temptation, she
swayed in the other direction, snatching in an audible
breath as she ripped herself from his hold.

'Like I said, I…need to think. I'm going to see Gianni.'

Without stopping for his response or to ask for directions, she flung her lithe, tempting body towards the door, leaving him standing there, a deep throb in his groin and the unsettling dread that he was falling under her spell…again…building in his chest.

For the second time in her life, Rocco Vitelli had proposed to her.

Only this time she wasn't the wide-eyed innocent who'd believed a candlelit dinner and a husky, accented proposal in a flower-decked courtyard of his Palermo villa was the start to her happy ever after.

Perhaps she should be grateful he'd spelled out exactly what his intentions were. Which were all about him and his grandmother and zilch to do with her emotional needs.

Not that she wanted him to cater to *any* need. Certainly not that insistent need that was making its presence felt as she attempted to smile for Gianni's sake, despite the fact that he was barely paying attention to her.

The housekeeper had found him a box of toys— apparently left over from her grandchildren's visit— and Gianni, content from a spaghetti lunch, was fully engrossed in it. Free from Rocco's presence, she had time to think.

Marriage. To Rocco.

For Gianni's sake.

Wasn't that what she'd wanted three years ago, even in her darkest moments when she'd feared she and Rocco might not settle their differences? For her child not to be denied its parent, the way she'd been?

So why did she feel this void inside her, as if something was missing? Besides a relationship with Gianni, Rocco was offering her career back. Another chance to fulfil the promise of both a profession *and* family, the way her mother had never been able to do.

For as long as she could remember, her mother's bitterness at what she'd deemed her unfulfilled potential at a career had been blamed on Mia. It was the reason she'd resisted the urge to jump straight into a family with Rocco when they'd first got engaged, despite the subtle pressures.

Fate—and a particularly heated bout of lovemaking where she couldn't remember whether they'd used protection or not—had found a way to settle things once and for all.

She had a son she'd never known she could love this much.

Rocco had the son and heir that he'd not so secretly craved. His grandmother had the offspring from her only grandchild. In essence, everyone would get what they desired if she married Rocco.

So what was stopping her?

Because you want more. She hid a grimace as the answer echoed in her heart.

No, she couldn't want more because more was *dangerous*.

My parents abandoned me when I was a child...

Mia's gaze swung to her son; she watched his profile, a younger version who would one day grow into the same formidable man his father was.

Could she deny him a chance to grow under his father's care?

No, she couldn't. She knew first-hand the anguish that would bring.

But marriage?

Her fingers shook, and she folded her arms to hide the trembling. It didn't mean anything, she assured herself. She would merely be another occupant underneath the roof of the sprawling villa in Palermo where Rocco lived with his grandmother.

Her lips twisted.

Most likely Rocco wouldn't even notice her presence, as absorbed as he'd become in his son in so short a time. Again that hollow inside her shifted, widened. Much as she wanted to dismiss it, Mia knew it wasn't that easy.

Once upon a time Rocco Vitelli had been the centre of her world.

Goodness, she'd even fancied herself in love with him. And, as evidenced, he still had sexual appeal she couldn't easily evade. But *she had* resisted him…

As she watched her son, her resolve slowly hardened.

She could do this.

That sexual weakness had been a temporary aberration, thrown up by the unsettling reality of coming face to face with Rocco after all this time. There were more important things to focus on. Gianni's emotional well-being. Her career.

And when the appropriate time passed, she would be free. She slowly breathed out. This was her decision, and she would make it work. Retracing her steps from where she'd paced to the window to stare out into the vast manicured garden, which seemed almost too good to be true in a property in Central London, she stopped beside her son.

Unable to stop herself from touching him, she ruffled Gianni's hair.

He looked up, a smile breaking on his face as he held up a toy. A red racing car. Mia smiled back, her heart filling with love all over again. If anything good came out of this, she prayed, let it be that Gianni would receive everything she'd been denied. To not experience the isolation she'd been forced to endure in her own childhood with a mother who'd laid all her hardships at her daughter's feet.

No matter how much she wanted to keep her son to herself, she knew that he would benefit from getting to know the Italian side of his family.

But before she gave an inch of ground to Rocco, she needed to put in a few contingencies.

She played with Gianni for another half-hour and then left him with the housekeeper and returned to the living room.

Rocco wasn't there.

About to go in search of him, she turned down the hallway.

She saw him coming down the stairs, a pillar of vitality and rugged handsomeness that stopped her dead in her tracks. Heat rose in her belly, and within seconds engulfed her whole body. He'd changed from the bespoke suit he'd worn earlier into a pair of stylish trousers and a polo shirt.

His hair was sexily dishevelled, as if he'd run his fingers through it repeatedly. Her fingers tingled, the urge to do the same overwhelming her for a shocking second before she wrestled the feeling under control. She might have had that liberty in the past, but no more. From here on out everything needed to be clinically platonic. She firmed lips that had parted at the sight of him, locking her knees as hawk-like eyes latched onto her.

She held her breath, delaying breathing him in as he stopped before her.

'Are you lost on the way somewhere or were you looking for me?' he drawled, sinful lips curved in amusement.

'We need to talk.'

One eyebrow rose. 'You've come to a decision so soon? I imagined I would be strung along for several hours, possibly a day at least.'

She shrugged. 'There's no point in delaying for the sake of theatrics. I've made up my mind.'

He regarded her steadily for a few tight seconds, his own breath seemingly held as he tried to read her. Then he nodded briskly. 'Come into my office. You can tell me what you've decided.'

He walked away, leaving her to follow.

His office was a masculine space, floor-to-ceiling bookcases interspersed with paintings and sculptures Rocco collected from far-flung places, turning the space from a simple office into a cultural and architectural masterpiece.

Mia wanted to stop and admire each piece of art, eagerly enquire of its provenance. Ask if their shared love of books had initiated this magnificent creation in the house he claimed he'd designed for her. She held her tongue. Because this wasn't three years ago. She might have given her body and what she thought was her heart to him a long time ago, but they were now strangers. Evidenced by the look on his face as he perched on the corner of his desk, arms folded, and regarded her with cool expectancy.

'Tell me then, *cara*, what have you decided?'

She held the decision tightly in her chest, debating the wisdom of her answer for one final second. But really, she had very little alternative.

She would do anything for her son. And denying him a bond with his father was unfathomable to her.

So, with her fingers bunched and her heart banging against her ribs, she announced her decision. 'I will marry you.'

A different sort of tension seized his frame, his nostrils flaring in the throbbing silence that followed. 'Repeat it for me, *cara*. Just so we're both clear that—'

'Don't pretend you didn't hear me. I said I will marry you,' she repeated, her voice firmer, resolute. 'But before you go crowing about getting your way, I have a few stipulations of my own.'

His breath eased out of him, his stance growing deceptively relaxed as he rested his hand next to his taut thigh. 'Of course you do. Perhaps I should be glad we're both laying all our cards on the table?'

'You should. I'm assuming we will be staying at the villa in Palermo?'

He nodded. 'When we're in Sicily, yes. But the villa in Rome and the apartment in Milan are still available should we need them when we're on business.'

She licked her lip, suddenly reticent about her demand. 'And…the Palermo villa…it's the same villa you owned when… I mean three years ago?'

'*Sì,*' he replied, his voice low and silky smooth despite the speculation narrowing his eyes.

Mia nodded, a little bit of the tension easing out of her. 'My stipulation is for separate sleeping quarters. I'm assuming you're still using the north wing, so I'll take the guest quarters in the east wing.'

He shook his head. 'That won't work. The east wing is currently occupied by Allegra and her children. And the west is still occupied by my grandmother. Unless you wish me to throw one of them out…' His voice trailed mockingly.

'Of course, I don't want that,' she said even while her stomach dipped alarmingly.

She'd wanted her living quarters to be as far away from Rocco as possible but even her first stipulation looked as if it was to be denied. 'We'll have to come up with something suitable, then.'

He rose from the desk, sauntering towards her with a gleam in his eyes that made her hackles rise. 'You agree to marry me in one breath then seem desperate to be as far away from me as possible in the next. Anyone would think you were running scared of something.'

She forced her gaze to stay on his. 'I don't care what you think. I just want my privacy.'

His eyes narrowed. 'Wanting privacy is one thing. Removing yourself so far away from me that it raises questions is quite another. Do you trust yourself so little?' he taunted.

'It's you I don't trust.'

He stiffened, his jaw clenching a moment before he spoke. '*You* don't trust *me*?' His voice was infinitely mocking, covered in ice. 'Pray tell, what have I done to deserve that distrust?'

'You really expect me to answer that? After throwing me to the wolves the very first chance you got?'

'I did nothing you didn't deserve.'

It was a testament to how unguarded she was around him that pain glanced through her midriff. 'One day, Rocco, I swear you'll regret what you did to me. If you don't, then you'll just confirm how heartless you've shown yourself to be since you threw me out.'

For the briefest nanosecond, she fooled herself into thinking she saw regret in his eyes. But then he shrugged.

'I've been called worse, *cara*. As to your request, if you feel that strongly about it, the adjoining suite to mine is still available.' He lifted his hand and ran a lazy finger down her cheek, leaving a trail of fireworks beneath her skin. 'It's yours to decorate to your heart's content until such time as you get over your false indignation. Then you'll know where to find me.'

She took a step back, removing herself from his charged orbit. 'That's not going to happen. Because my second stipulation is that you won't touch me again. Ever. If you want this marriage to happen, then you'll agree that it'll happen without any further physical advances from you.'

His eyes narrowed, and his hands dropped down to his sides. 'I seem to recall that you've come willingly into my arms each time.'

Heat surged into her face, his low, thickly accented words sending flames of shame and lust through her. Memories. 'They were temporary aberrations that will never occur again.'

'Never say never,' he drawled, a tight little smile

lifting the corners of his mouth. 'And be careful what challenges you issue, Mia. You know how very hard it is for me to resist them.'

She remembered all too well. Didn't he pursue her relentlessly for three months before she agreed to go out to dinner with him?

She'd got the job at Vitelli Construction after a gruelling set of interviews and she'd accepted with the sole aim of furthering her career and a determination to do nothing to jeopardise it.

The reminder of what her mother had endured as a single parent with zero career prospects, the accusations levelled at Mia for the simple fact of her existence, was the reason she'd vowed to herself at an early age never to fall under the spell of a man to the exclusion of all else.

But Rocco had very quickly consumed all her senses, his business acumen and his personal sexual charisma overcoming her every resistance. Those warnings had proved correct eventually. She'd lived in bliss for months, fooled herself into believing she was the exception to the rule. That she could have it all.

The reality check had been harsh and devastating. Within weeks she'd lost everything, save the new life she'd carried in her womb. She couldn't forget that abject lesson. 'So are we agreed?'

'Agreed that the physical side of this agreement will remain off the table until you come crawling to me?' he mocked.

'I won't. But if that's what will make you agree, then yes.'

His smile was pure shark, making her nape tingle alarmingly again. 'Of course, *cara*. If you insist.'

Refusing to rise to the bait he was setting, she turned to leave.

'That's it?' he enquired, sounding a little stunned.

She shrugged. 'What else is there? You wanted me to make a decision. I have. Now Gianni and I are going home.'

He was shaking his head even before she'd finished speaking. 'No, Mia. You are going nowhere. In anticipation of your agreeable answer, I took the liberty of getting my people to apply for a special licence. You will stay here with Gianni, and we will fly to Sicily in the morning. Preparations are already under way for us to be married.'

It was her turn to be stunned. 'How is that even possible? You've only known about Gianni's existence for a little over a day.'

'That should tell you how much I want him in my life. You've said yes so what's the point in delaying?'

The sensation of the ground shifting beneath her intensified. 'The point is that I have things to do.'

'Things like?'

'Like...sorting out my home. My life!'

He tossed her argument away with a very Latin gesture. 'My people will take care of that.'

'Take care of it how?' she asked, but she knew.

It was with the same head-spinning efficiency that he'd first relocated her into his life the moment she'd accepted his proposal three years ago. As a renowned architect, Rocco had exceptional focus and organisational skill that seemed almost godlike at times. His ability to create magic within a vacuum had inspired a following long before he'd reached his thirties, and the list of clients waiting for his creations across the world inflated his ego and multiplied his power. So why did he continually leave her slack-jawed by his ability to pull off something so simple as dismantling her life and rearranging it into his in the space of a day? How was she even surprised that he'd calculated the move a dozen steps ahead?

'Gianni doesn't have a passport,' she blurted, digging in as the ground gave way beneath her.

'That too will be arranged,' Rocco announced. 'Any other objections?'

A dozen easily rose to mind, but she knew that he would bat them all away with calm efficiency. And as he'd stated, she'd agreed to marry him. There was no sense in prevaricating.

'No. Looks like you're a few steps ahead of me. Congratulations.' Again she turned to leave.

'One more thing. I'd very much like to know why my son ended up on a billboard.'

She'd wondered when he'd bring it up again, wondered whether he'd condemn her for it, but his expression only held keen curiosity. 'Because it was a way to pass time.' And a way to earn money, which had been secondary but also welcome. Of course, she didn't tell Rocco that. She still had a little bit of pride left. 'And before you object to it, you should know, we worked with a very child-friendly agency and he was recruited by one of the mothers in the mother and baby group. There was nothing underhanded about it.'

'Did Gianni enjoy it?' he asked, stunning her all over again. From his reaction before, she'd been prepared for his condemnation.

Her insides unknotted enough to trigger a smile as she answered. 'He was the centre of attention, so of course he loved every minute of it.'

Her heart raced when one corner of his mouth lifted. '*Bene.* I'm thankful for the course of action that brought him into my life, but, besides the security risk, I'm also selfish and possessive about my son. So shall we agree to end the contract with the agency?'

She didn't owe him any explanation. That was why she didn't tell him that it'd only been a temporary thing. And of course, he was right. Now that Gianni had been claimed as Rocco's son, his father's wealth and influence meant his privacy and security were paramount. 'Fine. Are there any other edicts you wish to throw around?'

'You haven't lost your fierce spirit, *cara*. That's good to see. I have a feeling you'll need it in the weeks and months to come.'

'Is that a threat?' she asked sharply.

His smile widened, its pulse-racing effect making her clench her thighs tighter. 'No, *cara mia*, it's quite the opposite. Call it anticipation. Butting heads with me always turned you on. Seems you haven't lost that urge.'

Feeling another wave of heat invade her belly, she took a hurried step towards the door. 'I really don't know what you're talking about. Now if you'll excuse me, I'll go and inform Gianni that we're staying.'

He nodded. 'Has your email address changed?'

'Why?' she asked warily.

'To enable my team to liaise with you about packing up your house.'

Dear God, it was all going so fast. She raised a hand

to her temple and massaged it, hoping to stop the dizziness assailing her. 'I have a say in something, then, do I?'

Displeasure etched into his face. 'I'm not a complete tyrant, Mia,' he murmured.

You could've fooled me, she wanted to blurt. But she'd exhibited far too many weaknesses around him. 'It hasn't changed,' she murmured.

'Good,' he said abruptly, then, with another penetrative look, he turned away and sauntered back to his desk.

Mia left, reeling from the breakneck speed of events. Needing his grounding presence, she went in search of Gianni. She found him in the garden, exploring the profusion of flowers being tended to by the housekeeper. As if sensing she wanted to be alone with him, the housekeeper discreetly absented herself, leaving Mia to bask in her son's unabashed delight as he dug through dirt.

Hearing a plane flying overhead, Gianni excitedly pointed to it.

Unbidden, a lump formed in her throat. Tomorrow, her son would be taking his first trip on a plane. She stopped herself from telling him just yet. It wouldn't stop the freight-train momentum of what was happening, of course, but she needed a little more time where she could pretend everything was normal.

Eventually, when his exploration tired him out, Gianni crawled into her arms. She carried him inside, and, at the housekeeper's direction, headed upstairs to the guest suite.

Just like everywhere else in the house, it was opulently decorated. Thick luxurious carpeting muffled her footsteps as she made her way to an equally breath-taking bathroom. Every amenity had been provided, making her task of giving Gianni a quick bath an even more pleasant experience. After changing him into the lounge clothes she'd packed, she settled him into the multi-pillowed bed. She was barely a few pages into his favourite bedtime story before he fell asleep.

She was tempted to join him but the thought of Rocco coming in search of her made her reluctantly leave the room. Tentatively she made her way downstairs, only to discover that Rocco had left the house, with instructions for Mrs Simpson to feed her and a message to say he would see her in the morning.

Mia barely tasted her meal. For the life of her, she couldn't stop her mind from dwelling on where Rocco had gone. Which brought her to another matter she couldn't seem to stop her brain from dissecting.

Was Rocco seeking anyone? If so, how would it play out once they were married? He was a virile and passionate man, one who didn't apologise about indulging his needs. And since she'd effectively closed the door to anything physical between them, did that mean he'd cater to those needs elsewhere?

The bite of jealousy seared so deep, it killed the dregs of her appetite. What he did in his private life didn't… *shouldn't* matter to her. Just as she had asked for her privacy, she would turn a blind eye to his. Wouldn't she? But how would that affect Gianni? Realising she'd left one vital subject unexplored, she pushed her plate away.

Did she really have it in her to permit him to have liaisons with other women while married to her? The question kept her tossing and turning through the night, making her increasingly agitated and annoyed with herself for her inability to dismiss it.

This was a marriage in name only for the sake of their son. Surely what Rocco did outside ensuring Gianni's care and well-being was none of her business?

After repeating that hollow-sounding statement to herself a few hundred times, she finally got to sleep, only to awaken what felt like a handful of hours later to bright sunshine. Momentarily disoriented, she rose and rushed to Gianni's room, to find his room empty and a young girl, who introduced herself as Mrs Simpson's niece, making his bed. After she smilingly informed her Gianni was downstairs with his father, Mia returned to her room. As much as she wanted to storm downstairs and ensure her son was fine, she knew she needed a little grounding time. Plus a quick look in the mirror cheerily announced the effects of her restless night.

After a quick shower she donned the dress she'd worn yesterday and went downstairs to find Gianni and Rocco tucking into their breakfast. She stopped at the sight of them, her heart flipping over at the similarity between the two. They remained oblivious to her for a few seconds, giving her a chance to absorb their interaction.

Gianni was regaling his father with a rambling tale while attempting to stuff miniature pancakes and fruit into his mouth. Rocco was smiling, his attention rapt on his son's face.

An instant later he looked up, his hawk-like eyes locking on her. '*Buongiorno.* Are you going to join us?'

Gianni looked her way and broke into a wide smile. 'Mummy!'

Her heart filling, she approached him and dropped a kiss on his head. Taking the seat next to her son, she glanced at Rocco. 'Why didn't you wake me when he woke up?'

'We have a busy day today. I felt an extra hour or two in bed wouldn't do you harm.'

'Busy day?' she echoed as she helped herself to coffee. Rocco pushed a platter of pastries towards her. 'I thought your little minions had everything covered?' she asked, a little bitterly.

'We aren't just flying home to Palermo. When we get there you have event planners ready to liaise with you regarding the wedding. You are planning on being involved, aren't you?' he drawled.

That ground-shifting sensation returned. 'Is there any reason why we need to rush into this so soon? Can't we wait a few months?'

His eyes flicked to his son. When they returned to hers, their ferocity was intensified. 'I like to strike while the iron is hot, *cara*.' His voice was deceptively soft, for Gianni's sake, she suspected. 'And because I'd prefer my son in the rightful place that has been denied him since his birth.'

'Are you sure that's not your Sicilian machismo talking?'

He shrugged. 'Perhaps so. But I still want what I want. And I won't be denied.'

Before she could respond, a bell sounded. He tossed his napkin down, ruffled his son's hair before rising to his feet.

'That'll be my lawyer now. Finish your breakfast and join me in the study. There are some papers to sign.'

Mia blindly reached for her coffee cup, reassuring

herself that it didn't matter in the long run when she
married him. It was going to happen anyway, so why
not get it out of the way?

She ate her breakfast, then fed Gianni the last pieces
of fruit. As if by telepathy, Mrs Simpson appeared. Reluctantly, Mia handed her son over, and made her way
to Rocco's study.

The same Italian lawyer who'd questioned her at the
meeting yesterday greeted her neutrally, before produc-
ing papers the moment she settled in the chair in front
of Rocco's desk.

The twenty-page document was meticulous, outlin-
ing in stark detail everything she'd agreed with Rocco.
In return for marriage, she would get her previous position in his company back. The marriage would be
mutually dissolved once his grandmother's health was
improved or at such time as Gianni wasn't adversely
affected by a divorce between them.

Mia moved on, her stomach twisting weirdly every
time she read the word *divorce*.

She froze when she saw the sums detailed for her in
settlement for her future divorce. She looked up at him.
'I don't want your money,' she said, her voice sharp
and uneven.

Rocco's lawyer's eyes widened. He opened his mouth
to speak but Rocco waved him away. 'You will take it
nonetheless or there's no deal.'

She tossed the papers on the desk. 'Then there is no
deal,' she stated firmly.

This time it was Rocco's eyes that widened. 'You
feel so strongly about it?'

'I don't want *gold-digger* added to my list of apparent sins. I earn my own salary and when we're no longer together I'll look after my son with my own money. You can keep yours. Those are my terms, Rocco. Take it or leave it.'

His eyes narrowed into slits, his lips a flat line of displeasure. Before he could launch a counterargument, Mia reached across the table, took his fancy fountain pen, and drew a line through the offensive clause. After printing her initials next to it, she carried on reading, aware of the tense silence surrounding her. When she was done, and happy with the custody clause, which was most important to her, she signed the document and set the pen down.

Defiantly she stared at him.

Keen speculation gleamed in his eyes as he slowly reached for the contract. That gaze rested on her for endless minutes before he signed his name next to hers. Once the lawyer had witnessed it, he departed.

'If that was some ploy to make me think—'

'I don't really care what you think, Rocco. Not any more. Gianni's the only one I care about.'

A shadow crossed his face, a mix of speculation and suspicion. Unwilling to linger and be drawn into another charged argument with him, she left the room, went into the suite she'd slept in last night and gathered her things.

Five hours later—after a fifteen-minute video conference with expert relocators who had miraculously packed up her whole house and assured her her possessions were secure until she needed them—Mia struggled to keep an excited Gianni contained as they arrived at the private strip in North London. She explained to him what was happening as his father held him and, although she wasn't sure whether he'd fully grasped the unfolding events, he babbled excitedly as he was escorted in his father's arms up the short flight of stairs into the plane.

Once they were airborne, Rocco excused himself and occupied himself with business calls for most of the three-hour journey. He returned to where she sat with Gianni a few minutes before they landed, buckling himself into the seat next to his son.

Then he speared her with dark eyes. 'Your performance is about to begin, *cara*, so I suggest you compose yourself and stop shooting those dagger eyes at me.'

She inhaled sharply. 'My...what performance?'

'I've just been informed that my grandmother's meeting us at the airstrip. She couldn't wait to meet her great-grandchild. So prepare yourself.'

That was all the warning she received before she was flung into high drama that made her wish she'd taken another day, week or year to agree to this devil's bargain with Rocco.

Because it wasn't just his grandmother—leaning heavily on a walking stick beside the gleaming black limo—who waited for them when they stepped out of the plane.

Allegra Vitelli, Alessandro's very young, very designer-clad widow stood right beside her, one arm curled around the old woman's arm in comfort, while the disdainful glare she'd perfectly copied from her husband blazed from the eyes fixed squarely on Mia.

CHAPTER NINE

THE OVERFLOW OF emotion the moment Caterina Vitelli clapped eyes on her great-grandchild left a lump wedged in Mia's throat for a solid hour. She'd been prepared to defend herself and her child from even the merest hint of censure, direct or implied, but all they'd received since the swift journey from private airstrip to sprawling Palermo villa was unabashed joy, first from Rocco's *nonna*, then the household in general. Even the staff displayed wide smiles and open arms at being introduced to Gianni.

Mia's fingers tightened around the excellent glass of limoncello made with authentic Sicilian lemons they'd been served as part of what was turning out to be a lengthy celebration of welcome for the newest member of the Vitelli family.

For his part, Gianni was lapping up the attention.

A shame Mia couldn't relax long enough to even take a full breath. As she'd suspected, her child was being absorbed a little too eagerly into the family that had been denied him and was in the process of being spoiled rotten before her very eyes.

No, she had nothing to worry about in that department. But as one hour grew into two, Mia quickly re-alised she had everything to worry about in the form of the very carefully hidden contempt emanating from Rocco's cousin-in-law.

As if summoned by her thoughts, Allegra slid into the seat next to Mia. 'I haven't had the chance to add my welcome to everyone else's,' she said, her voice a sultry just-above-a-whisper murmur that Mia was sure she cultivated just so her companions would lean in to hear her.

She'd witnessed its effect many times when she'd been with Rocco. Not that Allegra needed it. She was the sort of stunning, statuesque beauty that stopped most men in their tracks.

'I could hardly believe it when Rocco informed us of the news,' she continued, chocolate-brown eyes siz-ing Mia up as she took a delicate sip of her sparkling mineral water. 'In fact, I'm still finding it difficult to wrap my head around it.'

Mia's spine tensed. 'I'm sure it all seems surreal to the outsider.' Hell, she was grappling with the fact that she was back here, in the majestic villa poised on a hill-side in Palermo, the place she'd dreamed of spending the rest of her life.

A tight smile curved Allegra's plump lips. '*Sì*, you're right. But I'm not an outsider, of course. I, like everyone else, found it immensely distressing that your child's existence was hidden from us.'

Your child. The stress on the word matched the sus-picion in the young woman's eyes.

'It wasn't by design. At least not mine anyway,' Mia responded, her voice a little sharper than she'd intended.

She grimaced inwardly when Allegra's eyes widened, sharp speculation gleaming in the depths. 'How very intriguing. What do you mean?'

Mia pressed her lips together. 'It's nothing that should concern you, I'm sure.'

Her gaze grew sharper, attaining malice that made the hairs on Mia's nape tingle. 'Oh, but everything to do with my family concerns me, Mia. I've learned to keep my loved ones closer, since the tragedy of my loss. I'm sure you understand.'

The lump in her throat dropped to form a rock in her belly. Was she being warned? 'What's that supposed to mean?'

Allegra smiled but never replied. Probably because Rocco arrived beside Mia in the moment, his incisive eyes latching onto her. But more than likely, Allegra had learned the art of subtle torture from her late husband.

Either way, she rose, swayed close to Rocco and laid a hand on his arm. 'Mia and I were getting reacquainted. It's good to see her looking so…well, again, *sì, caro*?' She flashed another sultry smile at Rocco before glancing down at Mia. '*Mi scusi, per favore*, I must go and check that the staff have done as I asked regarding preparing your suite, Mia.' With that, she set her glass down and strode off, her hips swaying with unapologetic femininity, leaving behind the unfailing declaration that she was the one in charge of the household.

'Is something wrong?' Rocco enquired after a tense beat.

'Why should it be?' Mia demanded tightly, unable for the life of her to breathe around the knot growing in her belly.

'Because you look like you're about to break that glass in two.'

She forced her fingers to relax. 'Can you blame me? This was never going to be a walk in the park.'

'Only if you don't allow it. Or am I misremembering that you thrive at the deep end?'

She bit back a snort of disbelief. 'We're not in the boardroom, Rocco.'

'No, we're not. And as far as I can see, you've been welcomed with open arms. So I ask again, is something bothering you?'

Mia looked towards the doors through which Allegra had departed, wondering if she was over-exaggerating what she'd sensed from the woman. She bit her lip and shook her head. 'No. Everything's fine. But I think I need to rescue your grandmother from Gianni's exuberance before he wears her out. He'll be a nightmare to settle down if he gets too overexcited.'

Her announcement was overly loud, she realised a second later.

A throb of silence went through the room. Then Caterina smiled. '*Certo*, Mia. Perhaps once you're settled in, you can let me know his habits? I would not like to upset his routine too much.'

Touched by the ease with which her request was granted, Mia relaxed. 'He's been resisting his naps lately, but normally he sleeps for an hour or so mid-afternoon, then has his supper at six. We…we can join you when it's time for his supper, if you want?'

Her hesitant proffer was greeted with a warm smile. 'I would like that very much, *ragazza dolce. Ciao, bam-*

bino,' she said to Gianni, who responded with a smile, albeit one worn around the edges.

Perhaps he was as overwhelmed as her because he didn't protest as Mia placed him in his bed ten minutes later.

'You have made my grandmother very happy,' Rocco rasped as they left a sleeping Gianni in the bedroom decorated with his favourite racing-car theme. Just how Rocco had managed to pull this off within twenty-four hours made her head spin.

'That was the plan, wasn't it?' she said, then immediately felt rotten. 'I… I didn't mean it like that.'

'Didn't you?' His voice was tight with displeasure, his hand frozen on the double doors that led to his private wing of the villa.

'No, I didn't. I just…' She shook her head.

'What is it, Mia? Are you going to spit out whatever's on your mind now or ambush me with it in another boardroom three years from now?'

She gasped. 'Excuse me?'

'I'm talking about your suspicions about Alessandro. And why you never told me.'

She rushed after him when he threw the doors open and walked into his private living room. From memory, she knew hers was the mirror image of the large, opulently decorated room, complete with the obligatory bust of some important Roman figure, a Renaissance painting or three, and the very best of mod cons. Heck, even the walls were lined in silk in Rocco's world.

'You're throwing the fact that I tried to spare your feelings regarding your cousin in my face?'

'Spare my feelings?' he asked, his voice chillingly

amused. He continued through his living room into hers, then into the bedroom, which had been redecorated since the last time she was here. Where there'd been pleasant pastel colours before, the room was now wall-to-wall virginal white from ceiling to carpet. Mia was wondering if this was Allegra's doing when Rocco added, 'I'm hardly a wallflower, *cara*.'

God, she remembered that all too well. 'Fine, if I'd come to you three years ago and told you your cousin was making my life a living hell behind your back, what would you have said?'

Without missing a beat, Rocco replied, 'I would've demanded an explanation from him.'

'Just like that? And if he'd denied it?'

'You're so sure he would've?'

'I don't know. But I didn't want to risk it!'

His face darkened. 'You didn't want to hurt my feelings or didn't want to risk not being believed? Which was it, Mia?'

'Either. Both.' She rubbed her throbbing temples. 'I'm not sure exactly what you want from me but it's a waste of both our time to second-guess the past. We are where we are.'

'*Sì*, we are.'

The change in his voice sent a different sensation charging through her body. That latent passion covered by the thinnest veneer of civility was rumbling again, like the not so dormant volcano this part of the world was known for. A single glance showed the innate sensuality was rousing, an uncoiling beast ready to strike.

For the first time, Mia became vividly aware of her surroundings. The vast queen-sized bed a few feet away.

The wide, sumptuous chaise longue, which seemed entirely adequate for a torrid tryst set before the perfect backdrop of French doors and the ocean beyond. The ankle-deep carpet beneath her feet.

Even the thought that Allegra might have picked every item in this room didn't stop flames from invading her belly, her nipples from tightening to painful buds as lust roared to life within her.

'There's one more thing we never got around to discussing yesterday,' Rocco rasped, sauntering towards her.

To step back would've exhibited weakness, to look away, the same. She did neither, even though she felt the ground tilt beneath her when he slid his hand over her nape, then up through her hair.

'What…what is it?'

'I allowed your wish to have separate suites. But outside this room we present a united front. No one, especially my grandmother, will know that our marriage isn't…for the lack of a better word, completely *fulfilled.*'

'Which means what, exactly? That I should pretend to be infatuated with you?'

A glint lit his eyes, wholly enigmatic enough to send frissons of excitement-tinged alarm through her. 'I wouldn't be so insensitive as to ask you for a performance you can't pull off. Attempting to withstand being in the same room without wishing for the ankle monitor you referred to should suffice.'

She hated herself for the searing bruise in the region of her heart at his rancour. 'I think I can bring myself to do that.'

His eyes narrowed a touch, then his gaze dropped to

her mouth. 'Just so we're clear, that may include physical gestures,' he rasped.

'Because you don't wish to throw your virile masculinity into question?' she taunted, despite every instinct warning her it was unwise to remain this close. To not protest the slow, hypnotic circles he was drawing on her skin.

'We both know I have no qualms in that regard. But just say the word, and I'll happily demonstrate.'

'No, thank you,' she said, cringing when her voice all but wobbled.

He leaned in closer. 'Are you quite sure?'

Mia cast around frantically for something to dilute this thickening fog of lust threatening to consume her. 'What about Allegra?'

He frowned. 'What about her?'

'Did we need to run our performances past her too? Because she seems to be running things around here.'

He shrugged. 'Allegra likes to feel needed. She never expected to be widowed at this stage in her life. She's doing what she needs to cope.'

Is that all? she wanted to ask. But she held the question in, part of her feeling ungracious at suspecting the woman's motives. 'Fine. Is that all?'

The question wasn't framed in a provocative way. But still it seemed to spark something to life. Something that needed very little in the way of kindling to come alive.

The very air seemed to consume her, even while giving her sustenance. She was aware her breath had shortened, her heart jackhammering in her chest. From the way Rocco's lips parted, the way his nostrils flared, he felt it too.

'Mia…' His voice was thick, throbbing with arousal. One that ricocheted through her with such ferocity, she nearly gasped.

Resist.

She jerked away, uncaring if the move was seen as weakness. 'I'm tired. I'd like you to leave, please.'

For a moment, he remained exactly where he was. Contemplating. Probing. And she feared he would call her bluff. Dare her to deny the dark magic spinning around them. Trouble was, she wasn't sure she would've been capable of it. She could barely recall her own name as it was.

Slowly, his hand slid from her nape. But he didn't remove his touch. Not until he'd drawn his thumb across her lower lip, something he'd loved doing years ago. A gesture perfectly aimed to remind her how the physical side of things had been between them.

'I'll leave you be, for now, *tesoro*. But *this* isn't going to go away just because you wish it to.'

'Then I'll simply file it under "the nuisance to be tolerated".'

He had the audacity to laugh. A wickedly husky, dark-as-sin laugh that stroked her in all the right places. 'And I'll enjoy watching you try.' His hand *finally* dropped. And she refused to admit she missed his touch as he strode to his suite. 'You know how to contact the staff if you need anything. Dinner is still served at eight. Nonna normally eats earlier but she's joining us tonight after we put Gianni to bed. We will give her the happy news of our impending wedding together then.'

* * *

Rocco didn't relish living in the state of perpetual anxiety. And yet he couldn't offload the sensation. But he absolutely refused to glance at his watch. He'd already done so at one minute past eight. That felt like…a lifetime ago.

'What is it, *tesoro*? You're acting like one of those feral cats that patrol the streets of Palermo at night.'

He would've been amused, and slightly disturbed at being referred to in such unpalatable terms by his grandmother, had his nerves not been so displeasingly frayed.

Mia was late.

She was never late. Or at least she'd never been tardy, either fashionably or otherwise, to an event when they'd been together. But then hadn't it been proven that he barely knew the woman he'd been about to marry?

She walked in a minute later, and he actively despised himself for the relief that oozed through him.

'I'm sorry I'm late. I decided to look in on Gianni.'

'Is he okay?' Nonna asked.

Mia smiled. 'He's fine. Wide awake when he should be asleep, but fine. I got pulled into reading him a story.'

He rose from his chair at the dining table and pulled out hers. 'That's good to know. I was beginning to worry you'd wandered into the sea.'

Mia stiffened. Nonna sent him a sharp look. Rocco hid a grimace, aware things were getting out of hand. Again.

Just as he knew the solution. An unbreakable commitment to secure his son in his life. For starters. Only once he knew Gianni was going nowhere would he be able to rest.

But that wasn't all, was it?

These fevered little incidents with Mia needed to be culled. One way or the other. And her wild accusations regarding Alessandro disproved sooner rather than later. His cousin had been hard-working, ambitious and fully dedicated to him and Vitelli Construction. The idea that he could've mistreated Mia, in any way, was deplorable to him.

And yet as he resumed his seat he couldn't halt the niggle of doubt that'd been resurfacing since Mia's declaration in his lawyers' boardroom.

Alessandro's not-quite-so-offhand musing over if Rocco was rushing his relationship with Mia

Alessandro's questioning Mia's credentials as an engineer.

He'd also noticed that when his cousin had been around, he'd demanded more of Mia than any of Rocco's junior engineers.

As if he'd wanted to see her fail?

He frowned inwardly, allowing Mia and Nonna to converse as he delved deeper into his memory. Looking out for his cousin and ultimate boss was one thing, but would Alessandro have deliberately kept him from his own child?

He shook his head, unable to fathom Sandro's reasoning for it. *If* he was guilty. The verdict was still out and he wouldn't rush to condemn his cousin until the evidence was before him.

'Caro? Che cos'è?'

He refocused at his grandmother's concerned expression. Mia, too, was staring at him but with less concern and more…indifference. That look grated. Resembled much too closely the one he'd seen on his father's face as a child. His mother's preoccupation with his father to the exclusion of her own son. Their callous dismissal of his very existence until their deaths and the realisation that he would never even know whether he'd ever been wanted. Whether he'd mattered in any way to them or merely been a biological accident they'd been saddled with.

He'd moved heaven and earth not to be irrelevant to anyone. That Mia would dare rake that particular wound—

'Perhaps we should leave him alone. It looks like he wants a meditative dinner rather than to be bothered playing host, eh, Caterina?'

The little challenging spark eased his tension, scorching away that unfortunate moment of self-pity. She wasn't indifferent to him. Hell, he'd stake his substantial fortune that it was the opposite. Still, there was a purpose to this evening beside breaking bread with the woman who'd betrayed him.

That urge to get beneath her skin sharpened. Without second thought, he reached for her hand, felt her tense at his hold and hid a smile. No, Mia was far from indifferent.

'I wasn't distracted, *cara*. Merely contemplating whether to deliver our news before or after we eat. And I've decided there's no time like the present, *sì*?' He raised her hand, brushed his lips over her knuckles. Relaxed even further when she trembled. Of course, confirming she wasn't indifferent to him returned him to that state of arousal he couldn't seem to halt whenever he was in her presence.

But that too would be handled.

'Che notizie hai?' his grandmother probed, momentarily forgetting that Mia wasn't fluent in Italian.

He switched his gaze to Mia, deliberately locking gazes with her as he kissed her knuckles again. Her breath shivered out, her expression giving her away. 'Mia and I are getting married, Nonna. And since so much time has been wasted, we've decided to wed immediately.'

His grandmother's reaction was gratifyingly warming. Rocco even managed to tolerate her tears and frequent bouts of excitement as the meal progressed. He barely tasted it, his gaze recurrently drawn to a solemn Mia.

Eventually, Nonna noticed too. 'You are happy about this, Mia?' she asked.

To her credit, Mia scrounged up a genuine smile. 'Yes, I am. But I wish I had more time to prepare though.'

He stiffened, but Nonna came to his aid, brushing away Mia's concern. 'Rocco is right. No need to delay this if it is what you both want. Plus you're wedding a powerful man. No reason why you shouldn't use his connections to ease your way in this process. I will of course help in any way I can.'

'Grazie, Nonna. As long as you don't wear yourself out.'

She waved him away. 'It was a little incident, nothing more. *Mio pronipote*, Gianni, has given me a new lease of life. Now, Mia, tell me everything you require and I will make a list. We will start early tomorrow morning.'

Rocco sat back, satisfaction easing through him as one box was successfully ticked in securing everything that was his. He was confident the rest would fall into place just as easily.

No alternative outcome was permitted.

Nine days after her arrival in Palermo, Mia stood outside the ancient double doors of a duomo a few streets from Rocco's villa. In terms of size, the cathedral wasn't large, but in grandeur stakes it dripped with history and prestige, from its golden, eleventh-century basilica to the carefully preserved mosaics, magnificent stone arches and Corinthian columns. It was also Caterina Vitelli's local church where she attended mass twice a week.

Mia's hand trembled and she couldn't quite catch her breath. While she wanted to blame the tight cinch of the corseted wedding dress, she knew it had nothing to do with the gown's design—which was a rich cream silk lace, sweeping, with a train stunning enough to render her breathless—and everything to do with the butterflies that had invaded her stomach when she'd awakened the morning after their arrival to Caterina's arm-long to-do list, and the reality that this wedding was happening.

Rocco, during their one and only discussion of the wedding, had acceded to her wish to keep it small. But Mia had quickly found out that *small* in Vitelli terms meant a few dozen people, because, while Rocco was Caterina's only grandchild, his grandfather had several siblings who'd generated a plethora of second and third cousins, most of whom were currently employed by Vitelli Construction. *All* of whom were eager to remain in Rocco's favour by honouring his invitation to attend his wedding.

One person in particular had been conspicuously absent in the last week though.

Allegra.

Apparently, she was visiting her parents in Northern Sicily with her children. The news had brought more relief than Mia was willing to admit. Nevertheless, over the past few days she'd grasped just how deep Allegra's influence went in Rocco's household. Each morning, there were fresh flowers delivered to every room in the villa as per Allegra's instructions. And Mia had discovered that most decisions concerning the running of the villa were approved or vetoed by Allegra.

Mia tried to tell herself she didn't care. But it grated to discover she couldn't request Gianni's favourite pasta be added to the shopping list without seeking approval from Allegra Vitelli.

'Mummy?'

She started and looked down to find Gianni staring up at her, impatience etched on his face. She'd given him the choice of standing next to his father beside the altar or walking down the aisle with her and her heart had turned over with joy when he'd chosen to walk with her. In his miniature version of Rocco's grey morning suit, with his hair neatly combed, he was too adorable for words.

'Shall we go in?' She infused lightness into her voice. He nodded eagerly, tugging at her hand.

She took comfort in his innocent touch, a mountain of reassurance in his unabashed stride as he urged her through the doors and down the wide aisle. Soft, indulgent gasps accompanied what was most people's first sighting of her son, but it did nothing to ease her nerves as those gazes swept up to probe her because the most probing was Rocco's.

Even from the distance between them, she felt its power, its laser-like, unwavering focus. It drew her like a magnet, propelling her forward until she was beside him.

Vaguely, she sensed Gianni being ushered away by his great-grandmother.

Then Rocco was taking her hand, firm and implacable, and turning her to face the priest.

The ceremony was shockingly quick, the words barely sinking in before she felt the soul-shaking finality of his ring sliding onto her finger.

She shivered; her fingers trembled wildly.

Rocco's grip tightened, his nostrils flaring in that possessive, definitive way that spelled that he'd well and truly captured her. Then he clasped her shoulders, tugged her to him. When their lips were a breath apart, he held her there, locked in his arms and by his gaze.

'You're mine now, *cara*,' he breathed, his voice low and for her ears only. 'Now show the world you're ecstatic about it.'

It took a moment to realise he was leaving the option to *her*. To buck tradition and initiate their wedding kiss. It was a clear challenge, a push for her to play her part.

Perhaps it was simply because this man drove her to dangerous extremes. Or perhaps because he expected

her to refuse. It might have had something to do with
not wanting to invite speculation from the dozens of
Vitellis holding their collective breaths.

Whatever it was, she refused to back away from it.

So she curled her hands beneath his silk lapel, slowly
slid her hands up to lock around his nape. Then rising
on tiptoe, she pressed her lips to his.

It was meant to be brief, to the point.

It turned out to be anything but. The moment her
lips touched his, Rocco took over. The alpha male who
couldn't cede control for longer than two seconds, he
slanted his lips across hers and deepened the kiss, his
tongue gliding between her lips to stroke hers.

The cheer of the crowd fell away, the rush of blood
in her ears drowning out everything save the riot of
sensation pummelling her. Time ceased to register. By
the time Rocco ended the kiss they were both breathing hard, his eyes dark and stormy as he stared at her.

It might have started off as a way to make a point.
But it ended with her recognising that she'd only weakened the armour she should've been fortifying around
him.

That thought triggered mild panic as Rocco escorted
her down the aisle and out into the waiting limo. As had
been prearranged, Gianni would ride with his grandmother and her retinue in another limo, leaving Mia
alone with Rocco.

She watched him reach into his breast pocket as the
car left the church to head back to the villa. When she
realised what he was holding out to her, her lips fell
open in shock.

She stared at the flawless, square-cut diamond engagement ring that had adorned her finger for many months before she'd realised she was living in a dream world. 'You kept it?'

He shrugged. 'I was tempted to throw it into Mount Etna at one point, but luckily I resisted that particular melodramatic gesture.'

Because he couldn't be bothered? 'Why? I'd have thought you'd be eager to be rid of it.'

His lips twisted. 'Perhaps I needed the reminder? Or more likely, whoever was tasked with removing your belongings thought it prudent for it to find its way to my bank vault. Which is where it's been all this time. Don't overthink it, Mia. You picked it. It's yours again now.'

He caught her fingers with his and slid the ring next to her wedding band. As if designed for the sole purpose of complementing one another, the rings fitted together perfectly. If he'd been anyone else, she'd have asked whether he'd intended it that way. But as he'd said, he'd barely given the ring, and her, a second thought until now.

She tugged her hand away and balled her fist, to hide its trembling and to hold emotions determined to overflow locked inside, while he sat back, his eyes resting on the rings for a moment before rising to her face.

'I take it from that smug expression that I've passed another one of your tests?' she asked.

'The one at the altar you passed with flying colours. For a moment there, even I was convinced we were an ecstatically married couple, crazily lusting after one another. So you see, *cara*, your transition back into my life is going to be less fraught than you think. And speaking of transition…'

The pause was deliberate. A predator taunting its prey. She knew it but still couldn't help herself. 'Yes?'

'We have an opportunity to kill two birds with one stone.'

She shook her head. 'I don't follow.'

'Nonna tells me you're struggling on where to settle on for our honeymoon.'

'I thought it better to appear indecisive than to burst her bubble by telling her we weren't going on honeymoon.'

A wicked smile curved the lips she could still taste on hers, causing her fist to spasm harder. 'Oh, but we've come this far, *amante*. We can't turn back now.'

Her heart did that crazy cartwheel again 'What's that supposed to mean?'

'It means, as of two days ago, I've officially signed on to build a performing arts centre in Macau. You'll accompany me when I visit the site. Nonna can be rest assured our marriage is off to a great start while she babysits Gianni. And you can dip your toes back into your precious career.'

'You expect me to leave Gianni behind?' she asked in surprise.

'We'll only be gone a few days. Besides, I don't think Gianni and Nonna are ready to be parted from one another so soon.'

It was true that her son and his great-grandmother had fallen head over heels for one another. But Mia had never been parted from him. 'I thought the whole idea behind this was so *you* would also get to know him, not swan off at the first opportunity?'

His face tightened. 'Like most working parents I

accept it's impossible to spend every waking moment with my child. How were you proposing to accomplish work and motherhood?'

She opened her mouth but no words emerged.

He sighed. 'I don't intend us to make a habit of it, Mia. And I will miss him too.'

She knew she needed to keep her guard up, but his words weirdly appeased her. She locked eyes with him for several heartbeats before she nodded. But when he reached out for her, she startled. His jaw clenched.

'We've arrived back home, *tesoro*. And we have a considerable audience watching our every move, so I suggest you put your game face back on.'

Her game face stayed all throughout the small but elaborate reception in the villa's lavish gold-themed ballroom—because Vitellis didn't do things by half measures. Through a stream of cousins, uncles and aunts whose names all blended into one after the first dozen. Through a first dance with Rocco while a renowned concert pianist serenaded them, when he held her far too close, murmured thickly, 'I think it would remiss of me not to mention you look breathtaking, *mia moglie*,' then delivered that wicked smile telling her he knew his effect on her. Through another dance where Gianni joined them, held between them as they swayed on the dance floor and Mia fought a different emotion, one that threatened to rip her heart in two because of secret yearnings she could never reveal. A yearning for these circumstances to be different. For them to be enjoying their son as a true married couple, with no signed agreements or restraints or bartering between them.

A dream that was destined to be unfulfilled.

'Mummy, Papà, dance!' Gianni cried.

Mia realised she'd stopped moving. As had Rocco. That they were locked in place staring at one another, with their guests looking on. She blinked, hastily erasing whatever emotion was laid bare on her face before she gave herself away. Then spent what was left of the reception wondering what Rocco had seen to make that contemplative gleam in his eyes flare for a pulse-racing, untamed second.

A handful of hours later, she drew in another half-breath, this one of relief as she bent over Gianni's bed to brush a goodnight kiss on his cheek.

'*Bella*, Mummy,' he murmured sleepily, stroking a chubby hand over the lace sleeve of her wedding dress.

For some reason, the words brought a tear to her eye. Or perhaps it was hearing him utter the Italian word. It wasn't his first. All week, he'd been repeating words Rocco had taught him. 'Thank you, my darling.'

'I see you're relentless with that charm offensive, *mio figlio*,' Rocco's deep voice murmured amusedly as he appeared beside her. 'But it's time to sleep now. *Dormi bene, caro.*' He leaned down and dropped a kiss on his son's head.

Another tear rose in Mia's eyes. She stepped back, blinking them away. Then she hurried from the room.

A few yards from her suite, she heard Rocco's footsteps behind her. She quickened her strides, eager to flee from him and from the cornucopia of sensation cascading through her.

Of course, he wasn't going to let her get away that easily. He'd sensed weakness in that moment on the dance floor. And, like a typical alpha warrior, was out to capitalise on it.

She threw open the doors to her bedroom, then turned, forced herself to stand her ground when all she wanted to do was back away, flee from that ferocious intent in his eyes. 'Did you want something?'

He smiled, lazily reached for his tie and tugged it off. He was the epitome of virile masculinity and suave assurance, and her already shortened breath strangled to nothing. 'I want a great many things, *tesoro mio*, but I suspect you might be more in need than I.'

'I haven't the faintest idea what you mean.'

He sauntered towards her, slowly winding the tie around his fingers before slipping it into his pocket. Then he nudged his chin at her dress. 'Your stylists helped you into that sensational contraption but I'm wondering how you intend to get yourself out of it,' he drawled.

Mia bit her inner lip. The corset was knotted in a profusion of ribbons at the back. It would take a contortionist act to free herself from it without help. But she didn't need the kind of help her husband was offering. Not when she didn't trust him. Or herself.

Rocco stopped in front of her. 'No need for such turmoil, Mia. All I'm offering is my assistance.'

A tight little laugh escaped her. 'Next you'll be asking me to believe in fairy tales where the big, bad wolf is just a friendly tomcat.'

He gave a throaty laugh. 'The only parallel to be drawn is that red *is* my favourite colour. But you're thankfully far from a guileless innocent, *bella mia*. And I have no wish to devour you.' He reached out, dragged a finger down her cheek to her throat, his touch testing her pulse. 'Not immediately anyway,' he added, a throb of unmistakable arousal in his voice.

'Rocco…'

He snatched her close, wrapping his arms around her waist. 'Give in to me, Mia,' he muttered thickly, his mouth trailing the sensitive skin of her neck, leaving a trail of gooseflesh all over her body.

'No.' The denial was weak, barely audible. So she tried again. 'That's…that's not what we agreed.'

Another kiss lingered on her racing pulse. 'The beauty of being adults gifted with reasoning and will-power is that we can change our minds. Renegotiate. You want me. And I need you.'

He pressed her closer so there was no mistaking the depth of his thick, powerful need. A helpless moan ripped free from her throat, ferocious desire mounting inside her.

'Are you going to deny this? Deny *us*?' he rasped fiercely.

Mia shook her head, more to rid herself of the fog overwhelming her than in answer. Vaguely, she felt his busy hands at her waist.

'Then kiss me, *amante*,' Rocco muttered, drawing back a fraction and holding himself temptingly just out of reach, just as he had at the altar.

And just as before, need shamed her resistance to smithereens, triggering a wild clamour that had her fisting his lapels and yanking his head down, her lips already parting as he hungrily bore down on her, accepting her greedy invitation to fling them both into madness.

And, oh, what sublime madness it was!

Mia couldn't get enough of his taste, of the thick arms that dragged her closer until they were plastered together from chest to thighs. Couldn't get enough of the rough sounds he made as he savoured her, his hands gripping her hips for a moment before he lifted her off her feet.

Her senses and body went into free fall when Rocco tossed her on the bed. He bore down on her, swallowing her cry of surprise with another torrid kiss that had her free falling all over again. Her fingers speared through his hair, gripping him tight to deepen the kiss. She moaned again when he wrapped an arm around her waist and rolled them over. Splayed on top of him, she felt a sense of feminine power and desire smash through her. She broke the kiss, awed and overwhelmed as their gazes locked. The surreal connection that had existed between them from the moment they laid eyes on each other returned in full force. Without conscious thought, she moved, dragging her heated centre over his erection.

Rocco groaned, gripping her hips to deepen the contact. *'Mia dea...'*

My goddess.

He'd used to call her that. She'd used to love it.

In the past. Before her life had detonated.

What was she doing?

Before she could course-correct, he spun them around again, resuming his dominant position and crumbling her resistance. This time, his hands wreaked deeper havoc, reaching beneath the silk and chiffon to brand her skin. Mia felt him tug at her underwear.

Then he was parting her thighs, sinking to his knees beside the bed.

Mia cried out in stunned pleasure as his hot, expert lips delivered a carnal, soul-searing kiss. 'Rocco!'

He didn't respond. He was too busy throwing her legs over his shoulders, parting her wider in order to drive her deeper into insanity. Mia was aware of the sounds emitting from her throat. Of her heart attempting to bang itself out of her ribs. Then, as he pleasured her with supreme expertise, she felt stars dancing at the edges of her vision. Right before she screamed in sublime release.

When she came to, he was kissing her fingers, her wrist, the oversensitive skin of her inner elbow. When he reached her shoulder, he murmured in her ear. 'Tell me I can have you, Mia.'

She opened drowsy eyes, stared at the stucco ceiling of her suite.

What was she doing?

The question came again. Starker than before. Reminding her how dangerously close she was getting to losing herself again.

'No. You can't.'

He reared up, mild shock tightening his features. His eyes blazed holy hell for a second. Then he launched himself off the bed. He dragged rough fingers through his hair, paced to the window and back. Then he speared her with an intense glance.

'You win this round, *dea*. But remember that ultimately I play to win. Make me suffer and I might just let you beg me for a victory.'

With that, he sauntered off, leaving her wound tight

as a drum despite the fact that at some point Rocco had achieved his purpose, loosened her corset and set her free from her wedding dress.

CHAPTER TEN

Saying a temporary goodbye to Gianni was heart-wrenching. It didn't help that he was completely oblivious, happily learning an Italian nursery rhyme as he perched on his great-grandmother's lap. Beside Caterina, Allegra's twin seven-year-old boys sat, playing on their tablets.

Mia was aware of Rocco's tense presence behind her. And of Allegra—who looked more as if she'd fresh returned from a luxury spa than from a family visit—lounging beside the massive mosaic-laid fireplace, her sharp eyes boring into Mia. She'd been surprised by the other woman's appearance at the breakfast table this morning, had known something was up with her when she'd proceeded to ignore Mia and converse in Italian with Rocco and Caterina.

But Mia had ignored her, preoccupied with the scene from last night that'd kept her awake long into the night. As she caressed Gianni's hair one last time, the morning sun glinted off her rings, as if she needed the reminder that the man prowling behind her was her husband.

The husband she'd displeased with her withdrawal last night. One who was still pissed off, if the turbulent look he'd levelled on her when she'd entered the dining room this morning was any indication.

'We're going to be late, Mia,' he growled, earning himself a sharp look from Caterina.

Mia rose, studiously avoiding him as she crossed the vast *salon* to retrieve her bag.

But contrary to hurrying her out, Rocco took her place, sinking low until he was eye-level with his son. She couldn't quite make out the words he murmured so she wandered out into the hallway, fighting back the stupid tears that threatened.

She swiped at her eyes, just as Allegra materialised beside her. Mia steeled herself to meet her chilling eyes. 'You think you're so clever, don't you?' Allegra hissed.

Mia stiffened in shock. 'Excuse me?'

'Making accusation about my poor Alessandro?'

Mia suppressed a gasp. 'How…? Who told you that?'

Allegra's face tightened. 'So it's true! You think you can take what's mine and soil my Sandro's memory in the process?'

'*What's yours?* What are you talking about?'

The other woman flicked a sideways glance at Rocco, long enough to ensure he was still occupied with Gianni, then stepped closer to Mia. 'I never thought he would be foolish enough to go through with this…*farsa*! But that was my mistake. One I intend to correct.'

'Do…do you mean my marriage?'

'There is no marriage, is there? Not when you didn't even spend your wedding night together,' she crowed.

Mia felt her face redden with humiliating heat. She didn't know how Allegra knew but she wasn't going to lower herself by asking.

'If you know what's best for you, you'll crawl back where you came from.'

Anger rippled up Mia's spine. 'Careful who you threaten, Allegra. You may have had your little reign here, but I'm effectively mistress of this house now. Which means I can kick you out like that.' She snapped her fingers in front of her face.

Allegra paled. Just as Rocco walked into the hallway. His eyes narrowed. 'Are you ready to leave, Mia?'

'Of course…*caro.*' She infused false warmth into her voice, her eyes still locked with Allegra's. The other woman's expression wavered, a flicker of fear in her eyes before it hardened again.

But when she turned to Rocco, she was soft and pliable, her sinuous body swaying as she pressed a hand to his chest, dropped a lingering kiss on his cheek and murmured in Italian.

Rocco gave a brisk nod, then catching Mia's elbow, he led her outside to the waiting car.

The first ten minutes passed in tense silence as she fought the burning sensation in her chest.

'Did you sleep well, *cara?*' he asked, his tone mocking the endearment the same way she had minutes ago.

'What do you care?' she snapped.

One eyebrow elevated. Then his mouth twitched. 'Shall I conclude that you didn't in fact sleep at all? That you're afflicted with the same discomfort I was?'

'Even if I believe you were in any way afflicted, you seem well on your way to resolving it.'

He frowned. *'Che cosa?'*

'I'm talking about Allegra. With her hands all over you. And you lapping it up.'

His eyes widened a fraction, then his smile returned. Wider. Deeper. 'Are you jealous, *amante mia*?'

Yes, she was. Wildly. Disturbingly.

'No. I'd just rather not be forced to endure the spectacle.'

'Rest easy. I have no interest in Allegra. I have no interest in any other woman except the one I married.'

She turned sceptical eyes at him. Then scepticism turned into shock as she read the veracity of the statement in his eyes. 'I…'

He made a very Latin gesture with his hand. 'You have locked us into this, Mia. I'll give you some time to get us out of it. But I won't wait for ever.'

'Wh-what does that mean?'

'It means I won't tolerate indifference, pretended or otherwise.' His tone was harsh, ringing with a deeper meaning that made her heart trip over. 'Deny this… *impazzata* between us all you like. But don't expect me to follow suit. I told you last night, I will win in the end.'

The warning was still ringing in her ears when they pulled up to the private hangar in Boccadifalco Airport. She'd been on the Vitelli corporate jet before and had always been overawed by the experience.

This time, however, preoccupied both by the little incident with Allegra and by Rocco's comments, and the fact that he seemed intent to delve straight into business, Mia had very little time to gawp at her opulent surroundings before they were taking off.

Soon after that, he turned to her.

'I have the blueprints of the project with me. I'd like your take on it. Shall we?'

She nodded, a thrill bursting to life in her chest as

she followed him to the middle part of the plane, where a large conference table and equipment had been set up for business. When she'd first met Rocco, and they'd travelled on his plane, she'd been concerned about the impact private jet travel was having on the environment. When she'd voiced her concern, he'd enlightened her as to the rigorous steps he took to offset his carbon footprint. And she soon discovered that every Vitelli Construction project was undertaken with materials that minimised its impact on the environment. It was one of the many reasons she'd loved working for him.

Within seconds of Rocco spreading out the blueprints of the proposed new performance arts building she saw that this was equally eco-friendly. In fact it was the most advanced ecological building she'd ever seen. Both in design and in implementation it was simply breathtaking.

After several minutes of absorbing the beauty and symmetry of his creation, she looked up from the blueprint to find Rocco's intent gaze on her, eyebrows raised. 'Initial thoughts?'

'It's…breathtaking.'

His eyes stayed on her for another moment before he gave a brisk nod. *'Grazie.'* The word was terse.

She sighed. 'I mean it, Rocco. This is magnificent.' The structure was designed to resemble a delicate brush stroke, poised towards an easel. The 'easel' was to be the main facility with the brush stroke containing everything from galleries to auditoriums, restaurants and a techno park for interactive play.

'It may be bold and innovative, but I need a structural engineer to show me how I can pull it off without it falling to the ground,' he mused.

She nodded, her eyes moving over the blueprint. 'I can give you an initial assessment once I see a feasibility report on the land and specifications of the actual materials we're using.'

Rocco handed her his tablet. 'The full report is on there.'

Their fingers brushed as she took the tablet from him. They both froze.

Rocco moved away first, firing questions at her as they examined the blueprints closer. He was halfway through another question when his phone rang.

'I need to take this.'

He moved away, and, eager to get started, she pulled up the two-hundred-page report. She was so absorbed she didn't notice he'd finished his phone call and was sitting across from her, intently watching her until she looked up.

Mia caught a naked expression of hunger on his face before he schooled his features, and other bout of heat flamed through her belly.

I won't tolerate indifference, pretended or otherwise.

His words returned to her, impacting deeper than she wanted them to. Had he been referring to his parents? She wanted to ask but wasn't she the one reinforcing the wall between them? What right did she have to personal details?

The plane banked slightly and again sunlight glinted off her rings. She stared down at her finger, wondering for the second time in a very short time if this was some sort of message. She wasn't one for flights of fancy, but since Rocco seemed intent on renegotiating their deal, was she foolish to dismiss it out of hand? Again she looked up at him, watched his eyes travel from her face to the rings and back again.

'Something on your mind?' he rasped.

She opened her mouth to say *no* but the word stuck in her throat.

What was she doing? She'd been married barely a day and already she was doubting herself? She pushed her thoughts away and glanced down at the report.

'The land is a little more waterlogged than I anticipated. You'll need more substantial reinforcement of the foundation to support the building. And the soil is also porous, so you'll require specially treated steel. I'll be able to give you a better assessment once we're onsite,' she said, striving for a no-nonsense tone.

A flash of disappointment crossed his face.

Had he been hoping that she would delve into the personal? With everything still so strained between them?

His expression neutralised, the moment passing. They discussed the Macau project in further detail, then moved to other projects he was working on around the world. Each one was a stunning work of art and she eagerly absorbed every detail.

Oh, how she had missed this. As much as she loved being a mother to Gianni, her work life had sustained her spirit, her contribution to transforming Rocco's vision from mere steel and bricks and mortar into beautiful works of art fulfilling in the extreme.

She barely felt time speed by but five hours later, when they reluctantly broke for lunch, Rocco tossed her an amused half-smile. 'You're enjoying yourself,' he observed, his gaze raking her face.

She shrugged. 'I can't deny that I've missed this.'

'Working with me?'

'Working at all. But since you're the only one I've really worked for, yes.'

Slowly, the amusement drained from his eyes. 'Then why did you do it?'

Mia stared back at him, praying he would read the truth in her words. 'I didn't.'

For what felt like a lifetime he simply stared at her.

'Do you believe me?' she pushed.

'Is it important to you that I do?' he parried, his voice thick with emotion she couldn't quite name.

She wanted to toss out a flippant answer to show she didn't care one way or another. But she did care. Perhaps much more than was wise. 'Yes, it is.'

'Then I will,' he stated equally simply. Starkly.

Her breath caught. 'Just like that?'

'The stalking case against you is fraudulent by all indication. It's reasonable to assume whoever went to the trouble set you up for the blueprints too. I don't need hard facts to tell me that. And in the grand scheme of things, no harm was caused by my opponents getting hold of those blueprints. They didn't have the expertise to pull out such a structure in a desert environment like Abu Dhabi. And once it became known that they were trying to pass off my work as their own, their reputation took an irreparable dent. If you want me to believe that you didn't betray me, then I will be prepared to put it behind us.'

A lump rose in her throat, despite the fact that he

hadn't given her the ringing endorsement of belief she'd sought. He was merely giving her the benefit of the doubt.

'What about Alessandro?' she blurted.

His features closed up, not before she spotted a shadow of doubt flash across his face. 'I will not rush to judgement until I have irrefutable evidence before me.'

She shouldn't have been hurt, of course. Still, her heart squeezed painfully. 'Very well.' She pushed her plate away, her appetite gone.

About to reach for the tablet to resume reading the reports on his various projects, she stopped when he brushed his fingers across her knuckles. 'It's time to take a break. If we don't want to battle jet lag when we land it might be a good idea to catch a few hours of sleep.'

Immediately her pulse leapt, her blood heating as memories from last night flooded her. 'I...okay, but not just yet. I want to finish this.' She indicated the report.

He stayed seated for a beat, then nodded. *'Bene.'*

Mia wasn't sure exactly what came over her, causing her to blurt, 'Why did you tell Allegra?'

He frowned. 'Why did I tell Allegra what?'

She exhaled. 'You said you didn't want to jump to conclusions or speak ill of the dead, but you told her that I suspected Alessandro was behind what happened to me.'

His frown intensified. 'Besides my lawyers, I haven't spoken to anyone about this.'

'Well, she knows. She accused me of sullying her husband's memory.'

'When?' he asked sharply.

'This morning. In the hallway, before we left,' she answered.

Fury blazed in his eyes for a few seconds as he wrestled down his emotion. Without another word to her, he rose and strode out, leaving her staring after him in confusion.

If he hadn't told Allegra, then who had?

Without a forthcoming answer, she refocused on the reports. It took precious few minutes for her to fully absorb what she was reading. By the time she was done, her neck was stiff and her back ached.

She'd barely managed to sleep last night, and her body was reacting to the adrenaline of re-immersing herself in her work. Shutting down the tablet, she made her way to the back of the plane where the master bedroom and bathroom were located. After using the washroom, she entered the bedroom.

Thick gold covers gleamed invitingly, sunlight slanting through half-pulled shades bathing the room in warm, enticing light. Unable to resist, she perched on the bed, kicked off her shoes and flexed her feet. Grabbing one corner of the spread, she tugged it down and slid between the sheets.

She meant to shut her eyes for ten minutes, fifteen max. When she blinked awake, the sun was setting and semi-darkness shrouded the room. But even in the dimness she knew she wasn't alone. She turned her head to see the dark figure heading towards the door.

'Rocco?'

He froze then turned around. 'We're not landing for another couple of hours. Go back to sleep. I only came to check on you.'

She sat up, relaxed against the pillows. 'Did you manage to get some sleep?'

In the darkness she saw his teeth flash a wry smile. 'At the risk of sounding like a broken record, sleeping comfortably when you're around has become impossible.'

She frowned. 'I really affect you that much?'

Again he smiled as he slowly walked towards her. Mia couldn't help but greedily absorb every animalistic movement of his streamlined body. She shivered at the intensity in the eyes that stared down at her when he reached the bed.

'You create a deep impact on me, *cara*. I've stopped bothering trying to deny it.' The words were thick, gruff, the hands shoved into his pockets attesting to the knife-edged control he balanced on.

Just like last night, feminine power resurged, sweeping through her veins like sweet, irresistible nectar.

'I believe it's why I reacted so strongly to the unfortunate incident three years ago,' he elaborated tightly.

'We're reducing it to one unfortunate incident, are we?' she asked.

One broad shoulder lifted in a shrug, drawing her attention to the fact that he'd discarded his suit jacket at some point and rolled up the shirt sleeves. 'I'm not interested in the past. Not any more. I wish to look to the future. And that future requires that we address this thing between us. I fear I will be intolerable if I keep losing sleep over you.'

She clamoured for outrage, but only ended up with breathless anticipation. 'That sounds suspiciously like another threat. I suggest you try harder to get some sleep. Perhaps you'll be less disagreeable.'

She started to turn away, but he placed a hand on her shoulder. 'Wait.'

Her eyes flew to his, connecting with the tempest raging in his eyes. 'If we can't indulge in one way, I'd very much like something else from you.'

'What makes you think—?'

She stopped when he placed a finger over her lips.

'Per favore,' he breathed.

Several heartbeats ticked by, all crammed with the urge to say no. But his gruff plea wrapped itself around her heart, and, as foolish as it was to let it affect her, Mia found herself nodding.

He didn't voice his request straight away. Instead, his hand moved from her shoulder, down her side to her flat belly, his gaze dropping to track his slow journey. 'Tell me about the pregnancy.'

Shock held her still. 'Why?'

His eyes rose to spear hers. 'My seed grew inside you, and you bore my son. Whatever went before and whatever comes after, it won't change the fact that the birth of my son is an experience I regret not sharing,' he said in a thick, charged undertone.

Having seen for herself how enamoured he was with Gianni, his pain touched her. Regardless of who was to blame for their circumstances, she believed Rocco would've liked to know about his unborn child.

Swallowing the lump in her throat, she let the memories flood in. 'I heard his heartbeat for the first time at nine weeks.' She smiled, her heart brimming with love. 'It was loud and strong. Funnily enough, it also made the atrocious morning sickness bearable. Be thankful you missed that part.'

Rocco gave a pinched smile and sank onto the bed next to her. 'On the contrary, I'm not thankful I missed any of it…but go on,' he urged huskily.

'Everything went smoothly after that.' Mia's gaze dropped to the handbag sitting on the floor.

Rocco's gaze followed, his eyes sharpening. 'What?'

'I have a picture of the ultrasound if you want—'

'*Sì.* I want. Very much,' he insisted.

She reached for her bag, taking out her purse and the celluloid frame she kept within.

Rocco took it from her, his gaze absorbing every inch of the black and white image. Perhaps it was the naked emotion in his face that prompted her next action. Reaching once more into her bag, she took out her phone, flicked through the photos.

He took the phone from her, flicking back and forth through the images taken by her grandmother in her cottage garden when Mia was in late pregnancy. Wearing a yellow sundress with her hair long and flowing, she was the epitome of barefoot and very pregnant.

After an age, Rocco swallowed thickly. '*Dios mio, eri squisito.* I would've given much to see you for myself like this. So ripe, so beautiful with my child.' His gaze lifted from the phone to her face. 'You cared for him in the midst of uncertainty and strife. For that, you have my thanks, Mia.'

His words triggered a shiver from temple to toe, in the process flattening her tongue to the roof of her mouth. Speechless, she watched him reach out and turn on the bedside lamp. She had nowhere to hide, but her body didn't seem interested in heeding her commands to move. So she lay there, her fists bunched in the bed covers.

Then, almost of their own accord, they slowly drew back.

Rocco inhaled sharply, his sizzling gaze scouring her body before coming back to rest on her face. 'Sleep will be the last thing we'll be doing if I get into that bed with you, Mia,' he growled.

'I know.'

Eyes locked on her, he toed off his shoes, then started to unbutton his shirt.

Mia swallowed, her senses jumping in a wild dance as she watched him shrug off his shirt to reveal washboard abs.

Dear God, he was glorious.

He paused with his hand on his belt, his eyes narrowing enquiringly on her face.

Her breath shivered out, ending in the low moan. And then she was rising, boldly placing her hands over his, brushing them away to take hold of his belt. Fingers trembling wildly, she eased it free, then slipped it through the hoops.

Rocco's breath hitched as her fingers grazed his thick erection. Hers followed suit at the realisation that she'd stepped on a roller coaster that would only have one heady, thrilling end.

Or a new beginning?

She pushed the thought away, too afraid to contemplate the future. She was living in the moment. Whatever happened afterwards, she would deal with that too.

'Do you intend to torture me to death with the slow teasing, *amante*?'

She looked up into his tense face, then looked down and realised that her fingers were frozen on the button of his trousers. Catching her lower lip between her teeth, she slowly eased it free, then drew down his zip. He gave a tortured moan, his hands jerking out to rest on her shoulders before sliding into her hair to grip a handful.

'Have your fun, *tesoro*, but do it quickly before one of us expires.'

She summoned a smile, caressing him with a light dance of fingers over his erection. 'Hmm, I'm almost tempted to see who wins this battle of wills.'

'Keep challenging me and we will find out,' he responded thickly.

Then in typical alpha fashion, he hooked his fingers into his waistband and dragged both boxers and trousers down. He straightened, his body on full, unapologetically masculine display as he stared down at her.

Swallowing, Mia looked down, her senses tripping over each other as she stared as his manhood—beautifully sculpted, virile and infinitely tempting. She couldn't help herself. She grasped him, then brought him to her lips. Another tortured groan ripped from his throat as she covered him with her mouth.

He allowed the caress for only a handful of seconds before he drew her back. 'Enough.'

Then he went on the attack, efficiently undressing her until she was equally nude.

Just like last night, he picked her up and tossed her back onto the bed. Without giving her a chance to recover, he prowled over her and settled himself between her thighs.

Rocco took her mouth in a hot, torrid kiss, delving deep and tasting her with the boldness that robbed her of what little breath she had. She clung to him, her fingers digging into his shoulders as she drowned in desire. They rolled from one end of the bed to the other, almost animalistic in their desire to extract maximum pleasure from touch and taste and the heady scent of their coming together.

Eventually, driven to the edge of madness, she broke free of the kiss. 'Please, Rocco, I need you.'

Her words triggered something inside him. Blindly he reached for the bedside table, pulled the drawer open and extracted a condom.

Rising onto his knees, he tore the packet open and slipped it on.

He was back, his fingers spearing into her hair as he angled her face up to his. Eyes locked on hers, he slid inside her. For five full seconds, Mia trembled, unable to stop the unrelenting tides of pleasure sweeping through her as he buried himself fully inside her. '*Dio mio*, you feel incredible,' he rasped.

She had no words to reciprocate. She could only moan in sublime delight as he began to thrust inside her. With each stroke, she grew wilder, clawing at him the same way sensations clawed beneath her skin, attempting to reinvent her very being.

Dear God, her memory had failed her. Because this was so much more sublime than she recalled. More soul-stirring.

From being on the edge of control when she was undressing him, Rocco seemed to have regained his will-power over his body. Repeatedly, he drove her to the brink of release only to slow down, fuse his lips to hers and patiently wait for the tide to recede before enacting the dark magic all over again.

Mia was sure she drew blood from clawing at his back, her throat raw from screaming her pleasure.

'I told you I would make you beg, didn't I?' Rocco muttered throatily when he had her poised on yet another peak.

'Yes,' she accepted. 'Please,' she begged. 'You win. Please.'

He held still, his lips a whisper from hers. 'This changes things between us. You know that, don't you, *mio moglie*?' he pressed, taking full advantage.

She didn't care. She was going out of her mind with this madness. 'Yes,' she cried.

'Just so we're clear,' he murmured, after pressing another hot kiss to her lips. 'No more separate bed-rooms, *si*?'

Mia groaned her acquiescence, her fingers digging into his back, her knees wrapped around his thick thighs as she ground herself into him. 'No more separate bed-rooms,' she gasped.

Triumph flashed over his face. In the next breath, his control snapped. His thrusts intensified, his face a harsh, beautiful mask of desire as he finally gave them both what they needed. Mia tumbled first, unheeding where she landed as she dived headlong into the most earth-shattering climax she had ever experienced. But through the fog of her bliss, she heard Rocco give a rough shout as he found his own release.

Sweaty, hearts racing, they collapsed into each other's arms and he rolled them sideways. He brushed his lips over her temple as they fought to regain their breaths.

Mia knew she needed to move, establish some much-needed distance, but for the life of her couldn't find the energy. When Rocco rolled onto his back and pulled her over him, she went willingly, her head resting on his chest as he toyed with her hair.

'I suppose you'd like me to do the honourable thing and restate my request now that I am not holding an orgasm over your head?'

She closed her eyes, revelling in the rumble of his voice beneath her cheek before raising her head to look him in the eyes. 'Do you feel like doing the honourable thing?' she asked, half teasing.

He raised an eyebrow and then shrugged. 'That depends.'

'On what?'

'On whether your answer will still be yes.'

Her senses screamed at her to be circumspect, to take a moment to reconsider what she'd readily surrendered moments ago. But she knew she was only fooling herself. She could only fight this powerful chemistry with Rocco for so long. At least on the physical side they were both equally bound by this spell. She wasn't fooling herself into thinking there were emotions involved. For as long as this chemistry raged between them, why not indulge?

'Contrary to what you accused me of last night, I'm not indifferent to the physical side of our relationship.'

An expression crossed his face, part triumph, part bewilderment. He didn't answer immediately, just continued to toy with her hair for another minute before he nodded. 'Then we are in agreement.'

She should've done the sensible thing then, just enjoyed the tension-free moment. Or, even better, encouraged him to sleep, thereby granting her some thinking room.

But Mia found questions crowding her brain and she let the first one slip out before she could stop herself. 'Is that what your parents did? Hurt you with their indifference?'

He stiffened beneath her, his face locking in a formidable rejection of her attempt to probe. 'What does it matter?'

'You seem hung up on it, that's why.'

His lips twisted. 'Aren't we all hung up on something?'

'I want to know, Rocco.'

His eyes narrowed into icy slits. 'Why? So you can tick a little feasibility box about me in your head?'

Her heart squeezed, mocking every intention to stay neutral. There was nothing neutral about what she felt about Rocco. Never had been. 'Don't do that.'

His nostrils flared, but he didn't respond. Not for the longest time.

When he looked down from the ceiling, his eyes were bleak pools of bruised hurt she'd never witnessed before. Her breath caught but she forced herself to remain still, not to offer comfort yet in case he withdrew.

'My grandfather left a sizeable inheritance when he died. With careful planning, my grandmother could've lived comfortably for the rest of her life. But my father coerced her into handing it over, with promises that he could double it. Within a year, he'd driven Nonna to the poverty line.

'Then he became obsessed with chasing what he had lost. He played the same game with my mother, frittered away her inheritance as well. The cycle just kept on repeating itself. Unfortunately for them, I came along.' His voice throbbed with bitterness but he clenched his jaw and continued. 'An inconvenience they tolerated up until the burden of having a child grew too much for them. They dumped me with Nonna and I hardly saw them more than a few times a month. When I saw them, my father would regale me with how busy he was. How he was taking over the world and how he would get back everything he had lost. Nowhere in that narrative did I feature. I remember wondering why he was bothering with me when clearly he didn't give a damn about me. Why he was torturing us with visits when it was clear he always wanted to be somewhere else, anywhere else but wherever I was.'

'Rocco...'

He shrugged away her sympathy. 'They died when I was seven. I remember that day clearly. The authorities arrived at Nonna's doorstep and I immediately knew. I told myself I didn't care.'

'But you did.'

He stiffened again, his gaze shifting away from hers to rest on the ceiling, but his fingers didn't stop playing with her hair. 'It doesn't matter.'

'Of course it does. Your feelings matter. You expected them to care for you.'

'Nonna provided me with everything I needed. More than.'

'But Nonna wasn't your parents. They brought you into this world. It's different, I'm sure, if you didn't know your parent at all, but to have them there right in front of you and still feel alone, unwanted or irrelevant hurts. Believe me, I know.'

His gaze dropped, latching onto her, compelling her own pain from where she had buried it deep.

'I don't know which is worse—having a full-time parent right in front of you who blames you for their every misfortune or having one who is occasionally present but distant.'

'Your mother.'

She gave a painful nod.

'Tell me.'

She shrugged. 'She got pregnant with me when she was starting out in her career. She wanted to be a nurse. But she was a young, single mother with no income to speak of. So she settled for…less. And she…hated me for it.'

Rocco frowned. 'Where was your grandmother in this picture?'

'Sidelined. For whatever reason, my mother refused all help. They fell out over my upbringing and never really healed their relationship. She seemed determined to lay all the blame on the timing of my arrival rather than…' She stopped, fresh anguish flaying her.

'Was that why you didn't want children?'

She tensed. 'It was why I wanted *to wait* to have children. I never *didn't* want children, Rocco. It was simply a matter of timing.'

Silence pulsed in the room, then he cursed under

his breath. 'None of that matters any longer, *sì*?' he said gruffly.

Something weighty shifted inside her. 'No. The moment he was born, Gianni became my everything,' she whispered.

They both stopped, absorbed the wonder of their child. From the first, she'd vowed to be a better parent. The way her mother had never been. The way she'd always yearned for.

'He makes me want to do things differently,' Rocco said gruffly, echoing her thought so succinctly her heart flipped over again.

Dear God, what was happening to her?

A lump rose in her throat and to combat the emotion, she simply nodded.

Then the plane lurched.

Rocco rolled them over and braced himself on his elbows. He stared down at her, but something told Mia the little heart-to-heart was gone. Certainly, the look in his eyes was no longer bitter, bewildered, or holding that hint of vulnerability she'd spotted as he'd spoken about his parents.

He was back in alpha-male mode, in control of everything around him. Of *her*. 'By my reckoning we land in about half an hour. This give us just enough time.'

'Enough time for what?'

He smiled, a wickedly male smile that reignited the fire in her belly. 'Let me show you.'

And he did, wringing cries from her throat as the plane started its descent. After another bout of lovemaking, they only had time for a quick shower before the plane landed.

Mia slipped into business mode as if she'd never left her role at Vitelli Construction.

The visit to the building site went off without a hitch, her initial assessments confirmed once she'd walked the ground for herself. The proposal to commence work in four months' time was signed off. Then she and Rocco headed back to their hotel.

The next three days flew by in a flurry of meetings, dinners with Macau city officials and clients. And to top each night off, mind-melting sex with Rocco. Private video-conferencing sessions with Gianni arranged by Rocco made the searing ache of missing him a little easier to bear.

They were preparing to go out to dinner with another set of clients the night before they were due to leave when Rocco excused himself to take a phone call.

Mia nodded distractedly, her gaze on her reflection in the mirror. Specifically, her dress.

The selection of outfits that had arrived from the exclusive boutique attached to the hotel, courtesy of Rocco's insistence, had been hard to choose from, each garment a little more perfect than the last.

She'd eventually settled on a sleeveless dark lilac silk sheath. But what struck her more wasn't the flawless design of the dress, but the renewed glow to her skin, the fuller curve of her hips and the vitality in her cheeks and eyes.

Observing the changes had quietly shocked her. Had it only been two weeks since Rocco charged back into her life? She'd changed inside and out, a realisation that triggered mild panic.

As she had been terrified of that first day, everything was moving too fast. But then hadn't it always with Rocco? Life with him was like a roller-coaster ride that could either stop at any minute or spin faster until you grew too dizzy to recognise your surroundings.

Was that what she wanted in the long term? She'd already abandoned her one stipulation not to share his bed. And how long would that even last?

Unable to face the questions darting through her brain, she turned away, slid her feet into designer heels that came with the dress and caught up her clutch. Leaving the bedroom of the presidential suite where they were staying, she spotted Rocco pacing the balcony. His phone was glued to his ear—a not unnatural occurrence since their arrival, but even from the distance, she sensed his tension. The sound of her clicking heels on the immaculate hardwood floor caused him to whirl around.

Laser eyes latched onto her, tracking her. When she reached the French doors, he ended the call and strode towards her.

'Is everything okay?' she asked.

'*Ovviamente.*' Despite his assurance, she couldn't mistake the terseness in his voice or his tense frame as he held out his arm to her. 'Shall we?'

She slid her arm through his, allowing him to lead her into the private lift and then downstairs to the restaurant where they were meeting their clients.

Rocco slid effortlessly into host mode. But throughout dinner, she caught his gaze returning to her repeatedly, the expression in his eyes unreadable. Her unease heightened as the dinner drew to a close.

Knowing she wouldn't be able to rest until she got to the bottom of what was threatening their albeit new but shaky status, she smiled at the client as coffee was cleared away, ready to make her excuses. But it turned out Rocco had other ideas.

'I'm eager to show Mia a slice of night life before we leave Macau. Would you care to join us?'

Mia barely managed to keep the astonishment off her face. 'You are?'

On previous nights, Rocco had bristled with impatience to get her back to their suite, barely waiting for the door to shut behind them before divesting her of her clothes.

Rocco smiled her way but it didn't cause quiet chaos in her. Probably because the smile didn't reach his eyes. 'We leave tomorrow, *cara*. We've done nothing but work for the past three days. I think you deserve to see something of Macau. After all, we have to report to Nonna when we get back, don't we?'

Of course. She'd forgotten that this was supposed to be a purported honeymoon as well as a business trip. Sure, the intimacy side of things had been thoroughly fulfilled, but she could hardly cite that, or recite the particulars of blueprints and steel samples when asked about her honeymoon, could she?

She let herself be ushered out of the restaurant and into a gleaming limo. Easy conversation flowed as they were driven into the heart of Asia's gaming capital. They alighted in front of a towering hotel, one of the many that had helped earn Macau the title of Vegas of the East.

A personal welcome from the owner of the hotel and the presentation of a huge pile of chips later, Rocco took over the blackjack table in the VIP section of the casino.

Mia tried not to gape in alarm as thousands of dollars changed hands at the careless throw of a dice. She would've been sickened by the sight but her husband defied the odds and, even in a game of chance, repeatedly emerged the winner. A performance that garnered a small crowd he seemed oblivious to, one possessive arm clasping her to him and the other tossing dice with reckless abandonment.

It was only when he caught her trying to suppress a yawn for the dozenth time that Rocco finally stepped back from the table and brushed a kiss across her temple.

'I think my lucky charm is done for the night,' he drawled.

Amidst good-humoured laughter, he took a hand, pressed a kiss to her knuckles.

Questions still teemed in her mind as they re-entered the limo, but this time, with just the two of them riding back to their hotel, Rocco had other ideas. The moment the doors locked behind them, he dragged her into his lap, sealing his lips to hers before she could utter a word.

As if he was on a mission, he didn't relent, drugging her with his kisses and greedy, fevered touch until they drew up in front of the hotel. Then he proceeded to slay her with passion, sweeping her off her feet, the moment they entered their suite.

An hour later, too exhausted to speak, think or even breathe properly, she fell into a blissful sleep.

* * *

Rocco stared down at his wife, guilt eating at him as he watched her sleep.

The phone call he'd received from his lawyers just before they left for dinner still sent shock waves through his system.

Alessandro had orchestrated everything.

His cousin had systematically and cruelly worked to hide the existence of his son from him, while attempting to bury Mia in a fraudulent claim.

Rocco could barely fathom it, had been reeling all through dinner at the thought that his own flesh and blood had gone to such deplorable lengths.

For what?

Power?

Had he not given Alessandro every opportunity? How had he found Mia so threatening that he had done this? Questions chased through his mind until they drove him out of bed.

Pacing the living room, he grappled with another decision.

He couldn't tell her.

Not yet. He'd only just managed to secure his position in her life. Discovering what Alessandro had done to her, to their son, might tip the scales into him losing everything. Everything he hadn't even known existed two weeks ago. He couldn't let that happen.

When the time was right, he would reveal everything to her. But not just yet.

More than discovering how much he'd missed the physical aspect of his relationship with Mia was the reminder of how much he'd missed her brilliant mind and her ability to see his work in a new light. Within three short days, she'd impressed his clients and team, both effusive with the compliments of her.

Far from having grown rusty, she'd delved back into a career that should never have been disrupted with an enthusiasm Rocco was nowhere near ready to lose.

'All I want is for my name to be cleared so I can get on with my life.'

Her words echoed in his head but he ruthlessly dismissed them.

He couldn't let that happen. Perhaps he was being underhanded and would pay when the time came, but that was a problem for another day. Hopefully a day when he'd reinforced the foundation beneath his feet with time and the promise of…

Of what?

A better future?

Why not?

His son was happy. Nonna was happy.

And he…was he happy?

Rocco couldn't deny that he derived a wealth of satisfaction from having Mia back in his life and in his bed. So…*sì*, perhaps he was happy. Thanks to his parents, he only had a barometer of what dysfunction looked like. Only time would tell how it all shaped up and, *accidenti*, he was going to take that time.

He crossed the living room to the liquor cabinet, and, despite it being the early hours of the morning, poured a cognac before returning to the bedroom. He slid in beside his wife, gratified when she rolled over and slipped effortlessly into his arms.

This was where she belonged.

This was where he would keep her. And when the time was right, he would come clean.

CHAPTER ELEVEN

Mia stared around her, the overload of glitz and glamour triggering a mild headache.

Monaco during Formula One weekend wasn't the arena for the faint-hearted. The billionaires per square metre was eye-watering. And with her husband easily part of the exalted club, the level of sycophancy was almost nauseating.

Of course she would endure it all, and more, to keep basking in the smile that was plastered on Gianni's face.

Her son had been beside himself when his father had announced at the breakfast table that, as part of his—week-long and counting—birthday celebrations, he'd been granted VIP status to the renowned Paddock Club in Monte Carlo.

But then in the months since his father entered his life, Gianni had been beside himself with joy on most days. True to his vow to be a different father than his parents had been to him, Rocco showered his son with his attention, their mutual love of fast cars only cementing their strong bond.

'Papà, look!' Gianni pointed to another sports car

from his perch on his father's shoulders, his eyes goggling in his chubby face.

'I see, *mio figlio*, I see,' Rocco responded with a grin, slanting a smile at Mia that, right on cue, set off fireworks in her belly.

She'd believed that the time before Rocco had cut her off from his life three years ago had been the most sublime of her life. She'd been wrong.

On the morning of their departure from Macau, she'd woken to a seemingly changed man. In all the right ways. Power and prestige had been a given in a life with Rocco. But the attention he'd showered on her and Gianni, the steps he'd taken to ensure her transition back into Vitelli Construction and the corner office that had come with her return to work had been mind-boggling. She'd quickly returned to being a valued member of his team. And best of all, oversea trips without Gianni had become a thing of the past.

To say her life had done a complete one-eighty was an understatement.

The only fly in her ointment was the delay in figuring out just who had tanked her life three years ago. And, for a man who demanded answers in every corner of his life, Rocco's seemingly relaxed stance in getting to the bottom of it didn't sit well with her.

Although…could she really blame him? Would she be in a hurry to discover if her own flesh and blood had betrayed him the way she still suspected Alessandro had if she were in Rocco's shoes?

Most likely not.

Nevertheless, the need for closure had been eating at her the last few weeks. Their conversation on the plane to Macau replayed frequently in her head. As much as she wanted him to believe her, Rocco had stated plainly that he wouldn't do so without solid evidence.

And more and more, Mia had felt as if without that, her life was on hold.

'Papà?'

'Sì, caro?'

'Can I have that racing car?' Gianni pointed predictably at a bright red sports car with Ferrari emblazoned on the side.

'Not that exact one, but maybe we can—'

She cleared her throat, shooting Rocco a pointed look. His grin widened, and her heart did that crazy thing again.

'We will discuss it when you're older, mio figlio.'

'Much, much older. Like when you're in your eighties,' she said under her breath, earning herself a low laugh from Rocco.

It was getting ridiculous how she'd begun to live for that laugh. For those smiles. Hell, how she'd begun to live for him full stop.

She didn't need to search deep to know that she had far surpassed the infatuation she'd felt for him three years ago.

Hell, who was she kidding? She'd fallen in love with Rocco somewhere over the Indian Ocean on the way back from Macau. So why did that make her heart twist each time she examined it?

Because she had no clue what he felt for her. He was seemingly content with their life together. The sex was beyond world-class. Gianni was thriving. Caterina's health had improved dramatically over the past few months.

And yet, every now and then she caught that tension within Rocco. And for the life of her she couldn't put her finger on it.

Her thoughts were still darting about when they eventually made their way to the VIP lounge. While Rocco and Gianni remained at the balcony to watch the race get under way, Mia made her way to a quiet corner of the lounge with her glass of mineral water.

From there, she watched, half bemused, as several women attempted to approach Rocco and were coolly rebuffed. Little did they know that no one came between Rocco Vitelli and his son. Did that commitment extend unconditionally to her? Or was she living on borrowed time until the verdict proved her guilt or innocence?

Unable to stew in the questions that had been plaguing her for weeks, Mia rose and made her way to the ladies' room. Exiting the cubicle, she stumbled to a halt when her gaze clashed with none other than Allegra Vitelli's.

Mia had been shocked when, on her return from Macau, she had been informed that Allegra had moved out. Rocco had seemed completely unconcerned by the development and, for a second, she'd wondered whether he'd orchestrated it.

She hadn't questioned it, had even been secretly relieved to be free of the woman who now glared at her with seething venom.

'I thought that was you, practising your…what do you call it?…chapel mouse stance up there in the VIP lounge.'

'It's *church* mouse, and you should've stopped by to say hello. I don't bite,' Mia replied as she walked calmly to the sink, washed her hands and reapplied her lip gloss.

The other woman's fury visibly grew. 'I don't exchange pleasantries with peasants,' she spat out, her eyes glittering like crystals.

'Well, then, don't let me stop you from leaving me alone.'

'Trust me I will, right after I set you straight on a few things.'

'Such as?'

'Did you not wonder why I left Palermo so suddenly?'

Of course she had, but Mia wasn't about to give her the satisfaction of confirming it so she busied herself fixing her hair.

'Not going to ask? Don't worry, I'm feeling generous. You see, for starters, your husband paid me a lot of money. Three million euros, to be exact.'

Mia's heart hammered in her ears. 'What for?'

'To buy my silence. But you see, I no longer need Vitelli money.' She flashed a diamond the size of a small country at Mia, her scarlet lips parting in a smug smile. 'I'm engaged to a charming French count and in the process of moving to France. So really, I've nothing left to lose any more.'

'What does that mean?' Mia asked, her stomach dipping wildly in alarm because all of a sudden she was one hundred per cent sure she didn't want to hear what the woman was dying to spill.

'It means you deserve to know the secret your husband is keeping from you. And you deserve to hurt the way your little reappearing act hurt me.'

'I'm not aware I did anything of the—'

'Oh, please, spare me the wide-eyed innocent act. You went digging in business that should've died with my Alessandro. And you turned up with your Poor Little Destitute act and stole Rocco from me.'

Mia gasped. 'You're deluded!'

Allegra shrugged. 'Perhaps. I'll never know now, will I?'

Mia bit her lip, but the question tumbled out anyway. 'What was the pay-off for?'

The cruel smile returned. 'To keep his little discovery a secret, of course. I heard the rumours and did a little digging of my own. So what if Alessandro took steps to keep Rocco from making a mistake with you? You were clearly sleeping your way to power. The child you claimed was Rocco's could've been another man's.'

Shards of ice pierced Mia's heart. 'You really think you can justify your husband destroying my life? So what, he could land a better position at Vitelli Construction? I wasn't his competition!'

'Not yet, but you had Rocco's ear.'

'And that terrified him so much he committed fraud?'

Allegra's face twisted. 'He did what he had to to protect his position and his family. You would do the same.'

'No, I wouldn't. And what exactly do you hope to gain by telling me this if not to see another family destroyed?'

Her eyes blazed with triumph before she shrugged coolly. 'We all deserve to know who we lie down with.

Your *husband* has been content to withhold this from you for weeks now. Maybe you should think about that?'

With that, she sailed out, head held high, blissfully uncaring that she, like her late husband, had shattered Mia's life.

For a second time.

Mia barely recalled making her way out of the ladies' room and out of the Paddock Club. Only had a vague memory of typing a hurried text to Rocco, informing him she'd returned to the hotel.

In the hotel room, she kicked off her shoes and paced, the ever-expanding pain in her heart demanding action. Rocco had known she was innocent all along and hadn't told her.

Why?

As if summoned by the single question blazing in her head, the suite door opened and Rocco walked in.

Gianni wasn't with him.

He pre-empted her question. 'Sophia took him to get a *gelato*.' His voice was heavy, his eyes intensely watchful. Sophia was part of the Palermo villa staff, who it turned out was specialising in childcare. A month ago, she'd been officially hired as Gianni's nanny.

'You know.'

He gave a single, jerky nod. 'I ran into Allegra. Or I should say, she ran into me. On purpose. Mia—'

'Why?'

He didn't answer immediately. He paced before her, dragging his fingers repeatedly through his hair until it was a dishevelled mess. Not that it reduced his hotness by even an iota. Damn him.

'You told me, repeatedly, that you wanted to put this behind you and move on with your life.'

'And you found that objectionable?'

He shook his head. 'No, I didn't. Only that I couldn't…take the risk that you'd move on…without me.' The words seemed ripped from his throat, but Mia wasn't in the mood to accommodate his discomfort.

She laughed. 'So you withheld the truth? Made me live with this hanging over my head?'

He paced to the window, whirled about and returned to stand in front of her. 'What would you have done if I'd told you on our last night in Macau?'

She gasped. 'That's how long you've known?'

He grimaced. Then nodded. *'Sì.'*

Shock threatened to weaken her knees. She sank into one of the many chairs littering the room. 'I don't know what I would've done. And I'll never know because you didn't tell me. You made me think that I had to prove myself to you. That I had to jump through hoops to earn your trust again.'

'No, it wasn't like that. I just didn't want to lose you!'

Her heart leapt, then dipped almost immediately. 'You didn't want to lose access to your son, you mean?'

'Don't tell me what I mean. You were what preoccupied my mind, not Gianni. You were the one I was afraid to lose. You are the one who has become as vital to me as breathing.'

She held up her hand, stopping the torrent of words. 'You know what, I don't believe you. Because you said it yourself, you play to win. Always. Finding out Alessandro did this to me put you in a position of weakness. So you withheld it from me. It's that simple.'

'Finding out my own flesh and blood did such a horrible thing to *us both* made me ashamed,' he bit out. 'He smiled to my face and stabbed me in the back. He did worse to you and, for that, I'm sorry, Mia. *Sono così dispiaciuto*,' he muttered thickly, taking a step towards her.

Again she held up her hand. Because something inside her was crumbling. And she couldn't afford to let it. 'Don't.'

For the first time in her life, she spotted naked fear on Rocco's face. He hid it well. In the bunching of his fists before clasping them behind his back. In the measured breaths he attempted to take while his gaze remained glued to her face. In the restraint he showed when she started to back away from him.

'Where are you going?' he finally jerked out when she grasped the door handle.

She stopped but didn't turn around. 'I've lived in fear for over three years. You can live with not knowing how this is going to turn out. See how you like it.'

He was in hell. Not just any hell. The special kind of hell reserved for *bastardi* like him who believed they could control the outcome of any event. He'd known the moment Allegra approached him with that cat-with-cream look on her face that his sin was coming home to roost.

He'd lied to the woman he'd never forgotten, the woman who owned his heart. All so he could hang onto her for much longer than he deserved. Just so he could try this *contentment* on for size when all along he'd known it was much more? That he simply couldn't live without her because he was nothing without her.

The next hour passed in excruciating torture, each second feeling like his last.

Rocco wanted to honour her wish to stay away, but what if each moment put her farther out of his reach? He'd never been one to sit and wait for things to come to him.

So, he wasn't surprised when his feet propelled him out of the door.

She was sitting with her back against the wall next to the lift, her head bowed. Rocco froze in place as she slowly lifted her head and speared him with eyes filled with pain and censure.

'You handled this badly, Rocco. So very badly.'

'*Sì*, I know.'

Tears filmed her stunning green eyes and he wanted to claw his own heart out. 'You hurt me. So much.'

Regret and fear shook through him. He swallowed both down. Everything was on the line. And now, more than ever, he needed to play to win. Deciding to risk it, he strode to her, scooped her up in his arms and returned to the suite.

And when she jerked herself out of his hold, he set her free. 'I swear on my life that I will never hurt you again.'

She shook her head, placing the length of the living room between them. 'I don't want that sort of promise. You can't guarantee that if you don't trust me.'

'I can and I do. Even at that first meeting in London, things Alessandro had said and done niggled at me. I didn't want to believe it. But on the plane when you asked me to believe you about the blueprints, I knew you were innocent of this too. But…we'd been barely been married for a day. We were so new. And what I felt for you overwhelmed me. All of this is no excuse, *amante*. But all I ask is that you give me chance to make things right.'

She brushed at a tear, and he felt it to his soul.

Dio mio, what had he done?

'How?'

'Whatever hoops you choose, I will jump through them. All I ask is that you don't leave me.'

'What if that's exactly what I want?'

He locked his knees to stop from reaching for her. 'Is that what you want? Truly?'

She didn't reply. But he spotted her fingers caressing her ring. Wild hope flared in his chest.

'What I want is…impossible.'

He shook his head. 'Nothing is impossible. Name it, *amore*. Speak the words and it will be yours.'

Her lips firmed for a long moment. 'I can't,' she whispered.

'Then let me speak them for you. You want to be loved—*ti amo tanto*. You deserve to be adored—you are my heart itself. I had no blueprint for love, *mio prezioso*. Not until you spread your love all over me and showed me just how sublime it could be. Even then, I remained blind. But I'm not blind any more, Mia. I might fail sometimes, but I will never fail at loving you.'

'Oh, Rocco.' Her voice broke, and, *sì*, he was *un bastardo*, because it was the most beautiful sound he'd ever heard.

Unable to stand the distance between them, he crossed the room and reclaimed her. To his eternal gratitude, she wrapped her arms around his neck.

They kissed long and hard and desperately, until she broke free. 'I'm going to hold you to that promise. You know that, don't you?' she whispered.

'I would expect nothing less, *amore mio*.'

Then, simply because he believed he would expire if he didn't kiss her again, he did.

But again, she broke free. He groaned, laid his forehead against hers, and just rejoiced in having her. His wife. His heart. In his arms.

'Shall we go and find our son?'

Rocco shook his head. 'Not until I've shown his mother just how much I love her.'

Her smile was wide, stunning enough to snatch the breath from his lungs. 'I'm not going to stop you.'

He swung her into his arms and strode for the master suite. As he walked across the threshold, she laid her hand over his heart. 'Rocco?'

'Yes, my heart?'

'Just so we're even... I love you too.'

EPILOGUE

Five years later

THE CLICK OF the camera's shutter roused Mia from a drowsy sun-drenched nap. Even before she opened her eyes, her lips were twitching with a reluctant smile.

'I should start charging you royalties for all these pictures you keep taking of me.'

Her teasing admonishing didn't detract her husband one iota. The moment she opened her eyes, he zoomed in, taking another lightning-fast series of pictures.

Only when he was satisfied did he lower the high-powered camera. 'Name your price and I will gladly pay it, *amore*,' he murmured, his avid gaze trailing adoringly from her unfettered hair, make-up-free face, and down her body to her belly, where Mia knew he would linger for hours if she permitted him.

At nearly eight months pregnant with their third child, she had very little inclination to do much besides laze about waiting for their baby's arrival. A situation Rocco took full advantage of, memorialising each moment of their summer break, including this private beach picnic at their Palermo villa.

He leaned down, dropped a kiss on her forehead, then traced a few more down to the corner of her mouth. There he paused, his gaze intense as he whispered, 'Call me primitive if you will, but I find you even more beautiful like this, with our child growing healthy and content, inside you.' His voice had grown steadily gruff and the kiss that followed lingered until she reluctantly pulled away, glancing over his shoulder towards the beach.

'Keep going and you'll scandalise the children.'

Rocco grimaced, then followed her gaze to where eight-year-old Gianni was patiently showing his three-year-old sister, Luciana, how to build a sandcastle. 'I will contain myself, for the *bambinis*' sake,' he grumbled.

Mia laughed. As if on cue, both children looked up and grinned. And, of course, Rocco raised his camera and snapped several photos.

She sighed in contentment, resting her hand on her belly as she mused in wonder over the last five years.

Save for a few bumps in the road, marriage to Rocco so far had been beyond blissful. The only trying period had been when Allegra's engagement had hit the rocks and she'd decided to sell Vitelli secrets to a tabloid magazine, fabricating a story about Mia's alleged clashes with her late husband causing her being disowned by the Vitellis.

Rocco, adamant about protecting Mia's honour, had given a TV interview, setting the record straight. And, before the whole world, had issued a heartfelt apology to Mia.

She hadn't even known she needed that last selfless act until Rocco had offered it, making their bond even stronger.

Her smile widened when Rocco rested his hand over hers, love blazing from his eyes when their baby kicked in response.

'No more pictures, please. Just sit with me,' she said.

He raised their linked hands and kissed her fingers. 'Anything for you, *il mio cuore*.'

Perhaps it was the hormones. Or perhaps it was the sheer happiness that often felt too big to be contained in her heart, but Mia felt tears prickle her eyes. 'You did it, Rocco.'

He glanced at her, one brow rising in the sexy, arrogant way that stole her breath. 'Did what?'

'You've kept your promise. Every day you make me feel worthy. That I matter. That our children matter. You've made us the centre of your world, and I adore you for it.'

He inhaled, heavily and shakily, his eyes growing suspiciously misty as he smiled down at her. 'I vowed to you that I would, did I not? I intend to keep that promise. In this life and in the next. Because, you see, it's quite simple, *amore mio*. You are my everything.'

* * * * *

WE HOPE YOU ENJOYED
THIS BOOK FROM
⊕ HARLEQUIN

PRESENTS

Escape to exotic locations where passion knows no bounds.

Welcome to the glamorous lives of royals and billionaires, where passion knows no bounds. Be swept into a world of luxury, wealth and exotic locations.

8 NEW BOOKS AVAILABLE EVERY MONTH!

#3853 THEIR IMPOSSIBLE DESERT MATCH
by Clare Connelly

A chance encounter between Princess Johara and a mystery lover was the perfect night. Until she discovers the man was her family's bitter enemy! Now Johara must travel to Sheikh Amir's desert palace to broker peace...and try to resist their forbidden temptation!

#3854 STEALING THE PROMISED PRINCESS
The Kings of California
by Millie Adams

Prince Javier de la Cruz's goal was simple. Tell heiress Violet King she's promised in marriage to his brother. His first problem? She refuses. His second problem? Their instant, unwelcome and completely forbidden chemistry!

#3855 HOUSEKEEPER IN THE HEADLINES
by Chantelle Shaw

Betsy Miller was ready to raise her son alone after tennis legend Carlos Segarra dismissed their night of passion. Now that the headlines have exposed their child, Carlos is back and everyone's waiting to see what he'll do next...

#3856 ONE SCANDALOUS CHRISTMAS EVE
The Acostas!
by Susan Stephens

Smoldering Dante Acosta has got to be physiotherapist Jess's sexiest client yet. Even injured, the playboy polo champion exudes a raw power that makes Jess giddy...but can she depend on him fighting for their chemistry this Christmas?

YOU CAN FIND MORE INFORMATION ON UPCOMING HARLEQUIN TITLES, FREE EXCERPTS AND MORE AT HARLEQUIN.COM.

HPCNMRB0920